Whites Only
In America

Whites Only In America
Copyright © 2023 by Artis Lee Holder

Published in the United States of America
ISBN   Paperback: 978-1-960629-10-4
ISBN   eBook: 978-1-959761-65-5

All rights reserved. No part of this publication may be reproduced, stored in a retrieval system or transmitted in any way by any means, electronic, mechanical, photocopy, recording or otherwise without the prior permission of the author except as provided by USA copyright law.

The opinions expressed by the author are not necessarily those of ReadersMagnet, LLC.

ReadersMagnet, LLC
10620 Treena Street, Suite 230 | San Diego, California, 92131 USA
1.619. 354. 2643 | www.readersmagnet.com

Book design copyright © 2023 by ReadersMagnet, LLC. All rights reserved.

Cover design by Ericka Obando
Interior design by Daniel Lopez

Whites Only In America

ARTIS LEE HOLDER

ReadersMagnet, LLC

Table of Contents

Introduction vii

Chapter 1:   Life in the Jim Crow South 1
Chapter 2:   Josephine Accused of Stealing a Dime 8
Chapter 3:   Mystery Woman Found in Chains 16
Chapter 4:   Jose's Childhood Secret 25
Chapter 5:   Return of Racial Threats 46
Chapter 6:   Jose's Memory Loss 82
Chapter 7:   Deidre's Obsession 106
Chapter 8:   Jose Has Doubts About Mullins 119
Chapter 9:   Jose Trap for Deidre 143
Chapter 10: The Groundkeeper's Death 163
Chapter 11: Deidre's Luck Runs Out 178
Chapter 12: Mother Daughter Reunion 182
Chapter 13: The Take-Down 191

Introduction

The title, **Whites Only In America**, was selected from a sign posted at the bowling alley entrance in Indian Springs, Georgia, during the civil rights era. This narrative tells the story of an elderly black couple who had been the handyman and housekeeper for the Kyle family since 1930. It tells the story of a horrible rape by a Jim Crow south employer that resulted in the birth of a child that the housekeeper would never hold in her arms. After waiting for over thirty years and hoping to see their child again, they decided to move to Florida and enjoy the rest of their lives. But now the housekeeper, Josephine, has been accused of stealing a dime in the summer of 1963. And their punishment was modern-day slavery. They were now forced to work for the Kyles and live in an old wooden shack.

Would they ever see their child again, or would the infant be buried among all the secrets of that old wooden shack where the abolishment of slavery was only a dream? Who knows? Perhaps *Whites Only*.

Chapter 1: Life in the Jim Crow South

The year was 1930 in Indian Springs, Georgia. It was a cold and windy night at the old wooden shack occupied by a young black couple, the Blackburns. They were handymen and housekeeper for the Kyles, who owned the wooden hut and the local bowling lanes, dancehall, and skating rink. As the young couple lay quietly in their beds, footsteps came at midnight, crunching the icy snow. Then there came a loud banging on the door as if there was an emergency. "Get up, Levi," shouted Mr. Kyle.

"I'm coming, sir," Levi replied as he opened the door.

"Where's Josephine?" Mr. Kyle asked.

"She's in bed, sir. Can I help you?" Levi replied.

"No, you can't. Just send Josephine up to the house."

"All right, sir," replied Levi. As Josephine lay quietly in the bed with her back turned and eyes wide open, she knew precisely what old man Kyle wanted. She silently turned to Levi while her facial expression spoke a thousand words. Finally, she said, "I'll go, Levi."

She quickly got dressed and headed for the main house. The older man was waiting at the back entrance when she arrived at the house. He grabbed her by the hair and led her into the employee quarters, where there was a small bunk bed. She began pleading with him not to bother her. "Please, sir, Mr. Kyle. I got my husband at home, and he gone be expecting me to do my business tonight, sir."

"Shut up, and do like I tell you," he said, as he ripped her dress open. He held his hand firmly over her mouth while he raped her trembling body. His only fear was that his wife would hear the screams and catch him in his evil act. Josephine lay there in silence, tears welling in her eyes, her body trembling with his every thrust. And without remorse, when he was finished, then left the room and never touched her again. He looked out the rear entrance window and saw Levi in the falling snow. He reached for his shotgun and put it over his shoulder as if he expected trouble from the angry husband. When he exited the rear of the house, he paused for a moment before asking Levi, "What are you doing out here in the snow, boy?"

"I'm waiting for my wife, sir," he replied.

"She'll be out directly," he said as he spat in the icy snow before walking to the front of the main house. Finally, Josephine exited the rear entrance where Levi was waiting to walk her home. But she walked right past him as if he wasn't there.

Nine months passed, and Mrs. Josephine was finally in labor and ready to give birth to her first and only child. Mr. Kyle called the town's doctor. When the doctor arrived, both he and Mr. Kyle walked into the shack. There they found Mrs. Josephine in her last minutes of labor. The doctor told her to push as hard as she could. "Come on, Josephine. You can push harder than that," said Dr. Lewis. Finally, after trying and screaming at the top of her lungs, the infant was delivered and began to cry. Mr. Kyle told the town's doctor that he expected it to be kept quiet. "You have to understand how these darkies are. Always in heat," he said.

"Yes, I do, sir. Yes, I do," the doctor responded.

The Blackburns were both fairly dark-skinned people, and it was obvious that the child was of a mixed race. It was considered a shameful event for a White person to give birth to a child with a person of color. If the delivery of this child had gone public, it would have been the end of respect for the Kyle family, especially since Mr. Kyle didn't even have children with Mrs. Kyle.

Mrs. Josephine, with tears running down her sweaty face, asked if she could hold the baby. "Is it a boy?" she asked.

"That's none of your business, Josephine, and I expect you and Levi to keep y'all mouth shut," said Mr. Kyle as he and the doctor left the shack with the newborn wrapped in a blanket. After they had left, Mr. Levi went back into the old wooden hut and closed the door. Then, with tears in his eyes, he walked to the bed to comfort his exhausted wife. They knew that there was no chance of ever seeing the newborn again. Never knowing if it was a boy or a girl, the Blackburns would suffer in silence for years to come. It was the Jim Crow South, and it seemed that slavery had never been abolished for the Blackburns. As the years went by, Mrs. Josephine would sometimes wonder where her child lived and if they had good parents.

As for Mr. Levi, he never knew if he or Mr. Kyle was his father. After all, it was the 1930s in the Jim Crow South, and Mr. Kyle was the grandmaster of the Ku Klux Klan. One could only speculate about what went on in the mind of Mrs. Kyle. There was no way for Josephine to know if she was even aware of what her husband had done or if she even cared.

Time passed, and in the summer of 1935, Mrs. Kyle gave birth to a baby girl, and they threw a party that was fit for a king. They had free bowling at the bowling lanes and free drinks at the dance hall for the entire weekend. After the party was over, Josephine was tasked with all the cleanings. While cleaning the baby's nursery, she couldn't help but notice all the lovely clothing and the fancy gifts. Seeing these things reminded her of the night she gave birth to her child, causing tears to well up in her eyes. At that time, Mrs. Kyle walked into the room. She held up her baby girl and said to Josephine, "Look, Josephine, isn't she beautiful?"

"Yes, ma'am. She is a sight to see, ma'am," Josephine replied.

"I was wondering if you and Levi were ever going make some little darkies," said Mrs. Kyle. "Of course, they would never be able to live here," she said.

"Will that be all, ma'am?" Josephine asked.

"That's all for now," said Mrs. Kyle.

While leaving the nursery, Josephine gazed sharply at the doorway she was told never to enter. She thought, "What could be the big secret behind those doors?" But, as tempted as she was, the fear of the old man Kyle was greater. One thing she knew for sure was that no one was allowed in that room. Not even Mrs. Kyle was allowed to enter. Then, one day, while cleaning, she heard a child crying. The sound came from the secret room, so Josephine decided to go closer and place her ear against the door to listen. As she placed her ear against the door, Mr. Kyle walked up behind her. "What in God's name are you doing?"

"Nothing, sir," replied Josephine. "I thought I heard a child crying, sir," she added.

"Well, you didn't, and if I catch you anywhere close to that door ever again, I'll put you and Levi in a pine box. You got that?"

"Yes, sir. Yes, sir," Josephine replied in a trembling voice. She could not help but think that the secret room had something to do with the child she and her husband had never been allowed to hold in their arms. But then, she'd never know because the following week, the door to the secret room was sealed, and an exterior door was installed. An eight ft. brick wall was also built to enclose the outer door. Josephine was not allowed anywhere near the house's rear side from that day forward. And those were the final words of Mr. Kyle. As time passed, Josephine watched as Kyle's little girl grew up. She would get her dressed in the mornings for school and walk her to the bus stop. She would be waiting at the bus stop for her return in the afternoons. Josephine gave her the nickname Tootsie, and she called Josephine Nana. Tootsie followed Josephine everywhere she went until, one day, Mr. Kyle saw little Tootsie talking with one of the black pin boys. He showed thirteen-year-old Tootsie how to grip the bowling ball, but little Tootsie had other plans. She began rubbing against Cane. She went underneath the bowling alley, and fourteen-year-old Cane decided to follow her. Tootsie whispered to him from behind the birdcage when he got under the bowling alley. As he was about to go to her, Mr. Levi caught him by the collar.

"What in God's name are you doing, boy? You trying to get us all hung?" he whispered.

"I ain't done nothing," Cane replied as he snatched away and ran back upstairs.

Mr. Levi looked at little Tootsie in disgust. "Go on back upstairs with Nana," he said.

She tried several more times to get close to Cane until they were seen talking together by Mrs. Kyle. That's where Tootsie's relationship with Josephine ended as her father forbade her from talking to any of the hired help. That included the pin boys as well as the Blackburns.

Chapter 2: Josephine Accused of Stealing a Dime

It was around 9:00 p.m., and the bowling lanes would close soon, so I went to turn in my game sheet for pay. When I got there, I saw Mr. Levi there as well. He asked Mr. Kyle if he could get his paycheck. "Not now, Levi. I'm busy," he said while sitting in his rocker drinking coke with his feet on the soda machine. His buddies just laughed. "Sir, my wife is outside, waiting for me to walk her home," said Mr. Levi.

At that time, Mrs. Kyle spoke, "Didn't he tell you he was busy? So get your black butt outside and wait."

"I was talking to Mr. Kyle, ma'am," Mr. Levi replied.

"You sassing my wife, boy?" Mr. Kyle responded.

"No, sir. No, sir. No such a thing, sir. I'm leaving, sir," said Mr. Levi.

"Come to think of it, where is Josephine?" Mrs. Kyle asked. "I put a dime on the table at the house, and when I got back, it was gone. So Josephine must've taken it."

"My wife ain't no thief, ma'am," said Mr. Levi.

"I'll settle the whole thing. I'm calling the sheriff right now," Mr. Kyle replied. He said it jokingly, but it was time for good old-fashioned nigger fun. "Tell Josephine to come in here, Levi. I want to ask her some questions about my dime."

"Okay, sir. I'll get her," said Mr. Levi as he left the office to get his wife.

Mrs. Josephine walked in with a big smile on her face. "How Y'all. Levi says Y'all want me to come in here," she said in a trembling voice.

"Josephine, did you steal a dime from my table today? Don't you lie now cause I'll kick you and Levi up the butt?"

His friends were all getting a big laugh from the horrible treatment of the Blackburns. Finally, Mr. Levi dropped his head and said, "My wife and Me gone be leaving now, sir, if you don't mind."

"Not so fast, Levi. I ain't done with you just yet," said Mr. Kyle. "Is that the sheriff out there?" he added.

"Yep, it's him," Mrs. Kyle responded with an evil look. "There you are, Sheriff. It's about time you get here," said Mrs. Kyle. "This nigger stole from me after all we did for her."

"No such a thing, sir. No such a thing," said Mr. Levi.

"Don't you be calling no White woman a liar, nigger," said the sheriff as he struck Mr. Levi in his head with the butt of his pistol. Mr. Levi fell to the floor with his head bleeding while the sheriff put handcuffs on Mrs. Josephine.

She started crying for Mr. Levi, begging them not to hurt him. She said, "Please, sir. Please, ma'am. I'll do anything you say. Just please don't hurt him anymore. Please, sir," she pleaded with the sheriff.

"Well," said Mr. Kyle, "there just might be a way for us to work this whole thing out."

"We'll do whatever you say, sir," said Mrs. Josephine.

"Well, I've always been good to you, Josephine, and it's only fair that you pay for your wrongdoings," said Mrs. Kyle.

"But I didn't steal your money, ma'am. I swear to God in heaven I didn't," said Josephine.

"Don't you use the Lord's name in vain, nigger," said Mr. Kyle.

"Tell ya what, Levi," said the sheriff. "If you and your wife are willing to work it off with the Kyles, then I'll work with you."

"Yes, sir. Yes, sir," said Mr. Levi in a trembling voice. "We're willing to work it off, sir. Just say how long we need to work, sir?"

"You asking how long?" Mrs. Kyle responded. "For the rest of your nigger life. That's how long. Or else carry Josephine to jail right now, Sheriff."

"No, sir. No, sir. We'll work, sir. Please, sir, we'll work. My wife is old, sir. She never means anybody any harm, sir," said Mr. Levi as he stood bleeding from his head.

"Go on. Git now," said the sheriff as the Blackburns left without their paychecks. I stayed curled up in the corner the whole time. That was the evilest thing I had ever witnessed, so I decided to wait and get paid with the others at closing time. When I got home, I wanted to tell my mom, but I knew she wouldn't let me go back, so I kept quiet. The next day, I noticed Mrs. Josephine was headed toward the office area. I ran over to warn her not to go there alone. "I'll be all right, baby," she said.

When she got to the office, she met Mrs. Kyle. "Get a bucket and some potash to clean up this blood Levi done spilled everywhere. And you better make haste. You hear what I say?"

"Yes, ma'am," said Mrs. Josephine.

I watched her as she walked away with her head down in shame. Shame and fear seemed to be a way of life for the Blackburns. I could never understand why they didn't just leave years ago. Maybe it had something to do with their hopes to find the child she had never held in her arms. But now, a prison sentence was being held over their heads for a dime she was wrongfully accused of taking. They were held captive by their Jim Crow employers.

Summer was coming to an end, and Mr. Levi had healed from his wounds. I decided to put extra polish on my lane to attract more customers. I worked hard to remove all the scuff marks from the white people lofting the balls. Lofting balls were against the rules, but they had a better chance of hitting the pin boy when they lofted the ball. As I was putting extra wax on my lane, Mr. Kyle came out of the office and called me to the red line area. "Yes, sir," I said.

"'Yes, sir,' my butt. Why the hell are you using my damn polish? I ought to kick your black butt," he said.

That's when something snapped inside of me. I was at the end of my rope. I walked over to Mr. Kyle and looked him in his evil eyes. I asked him why he hated black people so much. He just stood there and looked at me. I stared him down as I waited for an answer, but he just walked away, convicted by his hatred. Right then and there, I knew he was a coward. I went to check on MLK, my pet pigeon. When I got under the bowling alley, I saw Mr. Levi under the stairs with a toolbox. I hid behind the birdcage to watch what he was doing. He seemed to be putting something under the stairs that led to the skating rink. It was early morning, so I thought maybe he was repairing the steps before the customers came down. But as soon as he left, I went over to see what he had done. That's when I saw the fishing line tied from one side to the other. Somebody was about to have a severe fall, and I didn't want Mr. Levi to get into any more trouble. So I went over to look inside the toolbox for a knife to cut the line, but while I was looking inside the box, I heard Mrs. Kyle coming down to open the skating rink. I was too late. She tripped and came tumbling down the stairs. And immediately, Mr. Levi came out of nowhere, untied the fishing string, and ran off. Mr. Levi had also reached the end of his rope. He was finally fighting back with his evil tactics. Mrs. Kyle wasn't moving, so I called for Mr. Kyle upstairs. "What you want, boy," he said.

"Mrs. Kyle fell down the stairs, and she ain't moving."

He immediately ran down the stairs, rolled her over, and started calling for help. Finally, she sat up, and two other white guys helped carry her upstairs and out to the car. As it turned out, Mrs. Kyle had a broken hip. I only hoped she didn't remember the string. The fall could have easily been fatal for Mrs. Kyle, and Mr. Levi didn't even look back to see if she was dead or alive. Frankly, I don't think he cared. But now, Mrs. Josephine would have to wait on Mrs. Kyle's hand and foot. And when I say hand and foot, I mean hand and foot. One could only imagine how Mrs. Josephine would be treated staying at the house with that mean old woman day after day. But then my prayer to make more money was answered. Josephine couldn't leave the house long enough to get spring water daily. So Mr. Kyle paid me a dime a day to fill four jugs of water and bring them from the park to his house. Those were five-gallon jugs and very heavy. My fingers were numb by the time I finished. Of course, I had to make two trips, which seemed like three miles each trip. But I enjoyed my extra job because I got to walk Mrs. Josephine to the house each morning. One morning, Mrs. Josephine was acting strange, and I couldn't figure out why. That's when she told me that it would be her last day. She told me to always do well in school and to say my prayers. I was only seven, but I wasn't so naïve that I didn't know she was up to something. And I was scared for her because I knew she would be poorly beaten if she got caught with whatever it was. So I asked her, "Mrs. Josephine, what you 'bout to do? You know she's a mean woman, and if she catches you, she gone beat Y'all."

"Don't you worry none, baby," she said. "Just go fetch the water like they done told you."

"Okay, I will. But you wait for me to come back," I said. She didn't answer, so I was in no hurry to leave for the water.

While I waited for Mrs. Josephine to finish Mrs. Kyle's morning coffee, I peeked around the corner into the kitchen and saw her pouring something from a small dark brown bottle into the coffee. I knew it was something to make Mrs. Kyle sleep all day. But then I thought, if she wakes up, it's going be hell to pay for Mrs. Josephine. So I waited for her to take the coffee into the bedroom and set it on the bedside table. That's when I ran as hard as possible, yelling, "Snake, snake, snake."

I knocked the coffee onto the floor and broke the cup. "You stupid little nigger," Mrs. Kyle said. "You're gonna pay for that out of your paycheck come Sunday."

Mrs. Josephine tried to defend me, saying, "He's just a child. He doesn't know any better, ma'am. I'll clean it up right away. Right away, ma'am," she added.

When Mrs. Josephine kneeled to pick up the broken glass, Mrs. Kyle struck her across the forehead with a long metal hairbrush. Blood started streaming down her face. Finally, she stood up and said, "Will there be anything else, ma'am?"

Mrs. Kyle replied, "No, now get. And don't bleed on my rug."

As I watched, I thought to myself, I should have let that mean old woman drink whatever it was in that coffee cup, and as for the spring water, I didn't get any that morning. So I decided not to get her any more spring water. When Mr. Kyle asked why I didn't get water, I told him that my dad didn't want me to go to the park, which was the end of carrying water. It was also the beginning of a new life for the Blackburns as they finally left for Florida. They'd been wrongfully accused of stealing a dime and sentenced to a life of modern-day slavery. And now they were finally moving to Florida with relatives. Before they left, Mrs. Josephine whispered to me, "Keep your eyes open for my little girl because I know they got her in that house." So, as strange as it seemed, I did what she asked me to do. And to my surprise, while walking across the bridge, I saw a woman working in Mrs. Josephine's garden. When I told my Dad, he called the State police. They tried to verify the information by contacting the elderly couple in Florida. The relatives informed the police that they both had recently died together in their sleep. Their greatest fear of never seeing their child again became a reality.

Chapter 3: Mystery Woman Found in Chains

On Friday of that week, at precisely 1:00 p.m., the state police arrived at the Kyles' residence with a warrant to search the property. They knocked on the door. "What the hell y'all nigger lovers want this time," said Mr. Kyle. "Y'all done destroyed my business already."

"Sir, we have reason to believe that you're holding an individual here against their will," said the chief investigator.

"You need to go get a warrant, or else you need to leave my property," Mr. Kyle replied.

The state police presented him with the warrant and began the search. After about an hour into the investigation, one of the officers yelled, "Over here and hurry!"

A young woman was found asleep on an iron bed inside the old Blackburn shack. Her ankles had scars that had built up over the years from being chained to the iron bedpost. She was a beautiful woman who appeared to be in her middle thirties to early forties. When the state police asked her, "What is your name?"

She replied, "I don't know 'cept what Mr. Kyle calls me. He calls me Gal." She said, "He moved me out here in this shack when his workers left."

The police took her to the van. When the others saw the woman and heard her story, there wasn't a dry eye on the yard as they put her into the van. Mr. Kyle was handcuffed and taken into custody.

Mrs. Kyle came out of the house, yelling at the police, "Where the hell are Y'all taking him? Get off my land!"

"Don't worry, ma'am," said the chief investigator. "You're going with him because you're just as guilty. Cuff her."

As they arrived at the Butts County jail, the sheriff came out. "What the hell Y'all doing in my county, arresting my citizens?" he asked.

"If you must know, your citizens are being charged with kidnapping and who knows what else. Just make damn sure you're not involved, Sheriff. Now book them, not in the same cell," said the investigator. "I've got a lot more interrogating to do, and I'm just getting started."

"Tell me something, Sheriff," said Officer Mullins. "Were you aware that this woman even existed?" He paused for a moment, then shook his head. Then, while walking away, he turned to the Sheriff and said, "You better hope Chief doesn't find that you're involved. Because if he does, they need a Mack truck to pull his foot from your behind. And that, sir, you can count on." Officer Mullins was the only black officer on the investigation team.

As for the Kyles', they didn't get separate cells because they were signed out on bond almost immediately when their attorney arrived. "I'll have your badge, you stinking nigger lover. You wait and see," said Mr. Kyle as he left the jail, pointing his finger at the chief investigator.

As for the nameless woman rescued from Kyle's property and into protective custody, rumors began to travel throughout the black and white communities about the woman who lived on Kyle's property without a name. They even spread rumors that wild animals raised her. There were reporters from as far away as South Carolina and Florida who wanted interviews with the mystery woman.

They even camped out at the Kyles' place, hoping to get a comment from either Mr. or Mrs. Kyle. A reporter from Atlanta finally went to the black community, hoping to get an exclusive with the neighborhood watch group. He asked around until he finally concluded that no one was going to trust anyone who was white. So he decided to settle for some photos for his story. He drove through the community and took several pictures before being stopped by Clem. "Hey, man, can I help you with something?" Clem asked.

"Well, I was hoping to get you people's side of the story about the woman found at the Kyles' place," he said.

"What's your name, and who are you working with?" Clem asked.

"My name is Billy Williams, and I'm with the *Daily News* out of Charleston, South Carolina."

"Well, park the car and get out. And if I find out you're working for Kyle, then you're on your own. "People are pretty stirred up about old man Kyle locking that young girl up the way he did." Billy replied, "We want to give you and the people in this county a voice come trial time. Now I know that's a long shot when discussing getting a fair trial in the South. But I'm willing to give it a shot if you are."

"I'll have to discuss it with the community before I say anything definite, but I think we might just take you up on the offer," said Clem.

After the reporter left, Clem called up some of the guys and told them about the reporter. They decided it would be better to ask Officer Mullins if he thought it might jeopardize the Kyle case. Officer Mullins told Clem that it would not be wise to give any information to anyone at that time. And that was the end for the reporter in the black community. The reporter's offer was declined, and the community would wait for answers concerning the woman found in chains.

But all of that would soon be laid to rest as the trial date finally arrived. People of all races gathered around the courthouse square as Mr. and Mrs. Kyle arrived with their attorney. As they walked up to the courthouse, members of the white community cheered them on. They yelled things like, "Go get those nigger lovers."

The blacks remained silent as they watched in anger. They knew that the county police would like nothing more than to arrest them for disturbing the peace. The only people allowed inside the courtroom were whites and selected blacks. The jury was preselected and all white. The Kyles pleaded not guilty to the charges. It took a jury less than thirty minutes to return with a not-guilty verdict, which was not unusual for that courthouse. After all, they still had the signs posted on the water fountains and restrooms, Whites Only. Imagine that five years after the Civil Rights Act.

After the verdict was read, all twelve jurors came over to celebrate the victory with the Kyles. "I told you not to worry about a damn thang," the Jury Chairman said. Officer Mullins overheard the comment, so he approached the juror and whispered in his ear, "I'll show you who's the monkey, and you can bank on it, mister," said Officer Mullins in anger over the thirty-minute all-white verdict. Nevertheless, it was determined by the courts that the woman on the Kyle property was the daughter of Mrs. Josephine Blackburn. They refused to give the biological father's name, but the townspeople had a good idea that old man Kyle had something to do with it.

The woman named Gal explained to the courts that she had lived in the rear of the Kyle home as far back as she could remember but was never allowed to play out front. She stated she prepared meals in her room, and all of her needs, including toys, had been supplied over the years by Mr. and Mrs. Kyle. That would prove to be the reason for not allowing the housekeeper to enter that part of the house. It also proved that Mrs. Kyle knew Josephine's child was there all along. It was a heartless thing for one mother to do to another mother. And it explained why Mrs. Kyle made racist comments at her daughter's first birthday party. She told Mrs. Josephine that her darkies would never be able to live at her home when she knew the child was already locked away in that horrible room. How did she explain that to her daughter, Mildred?

The blacks began to shout out when the verdict was announced outside the courtroom. Then, they all chanted, "We want justice" repeatedly.

The county police must have known the verdict because the National Guard was already standing by. They surrounded the courthouse square in less than five minutes, along with the county and city police. They were prepared with attack dogs and large water hoses. But the blacks would prove far more intelligent than the law enforcement agencies. They had received training from the NAACP (National Association for the Advancement of Colored People) on conducting non-violent rallies.

As for the Kyles, they came out of the courthouse with relief. "I done said it once, and I'll repeat it, ain't no nigger-loving Yankee gone tell me how to live or who to live with," said Mr. Kyle. They had won their case in court with a twelve-man jury and a judge who was a relative of Kyle's family. It had to be evident because his name was Judge Joe Kyle. He and Mr. Kyle were the sons of two brothers.

That was a tremendous blow to race relations in the small town of Jackson. After all, it was 1970 in the South. Then, finally, the young woman came out of the courtroom. Everyone watched in silence as she approached the state police vehicle. She had been secretly brought into the courtroom for her safety and because of all the rumors about her being some wild woman. The town would be waiting in suspense to hear her speak for the first time. Then, finally, all black and white people would listen to and see what racism had done to that human being.

At first, she stayed silent as if she were afraid. She looked over at the Kyles as they celebrated their victory. And then she spoke. "I'm glad to be free." She turned away and got into the state police van.

"Oh my god, Daddy," said Mildred to her father, Mr. Kyle. "What have you done, Daddy? What have you done?"

Mildred suddenly remembered her Nana, Josephine, from her childhood. And now, knowing that Josephine was that woman's mother, she wondered why it was so secret and why she was locked away.

"Did you lock my sister up like an animal? Daddy, what have you done?"

"Let's go, honey," said Wally to Mildred.

"Leave me the hell alone, Wally," said Mildred as her father hurried into his truck with Mrs. Kyle. "You will talk to me, Daddy, and you can count on it," Mildred said.

"Honey," said Wally.

"This is not the time, Wally," she said as she stomped to their car. "Come on, Wally," she shouted. Mildred was both angry and confused. The young woman chained in the old wooden shack looked almost identical to Mr. Kyle's daughter, Mildred.

And all of the townspeople saw the stunning resemblance and began to mumble among themselves. Finally, one woman said to her husband, "Is that woman a nigger, or is she white?" No one knew for sure, but all bets were on Mr. Kyle being the biological father.

She was taken to a wellness clinic, where she learned to read, write, and, more importantly, live a healthy and fruitful life. It was a difficult task that lasted almost two years, but she was determined to succeed. After being called gal her entire life, she adopted her mother's name, Jose Blackburn. She had formed her first real relationship with Officer Mullins, and he promised to stay by her side. That promise led to the beginning of a happy life together. They were married shortly after, with Jose giving birth to a baby boy. They named him Levi as a reminder of the Father she never knew. Officer Mullins had found the love of his life. Jose progressed well at the Learning Center but was still cautious around crowds. Would she ever fully recover? Who knows? Perhaps Whites Only.

Chapter 4: Jose's Childhood Secret

Three years later

Just when you thought it couldn't get any worse, Officer Mullins received disturbing news concerning his beautiful wife, Jose. It had been only three years since her rescue from a horrible life of captivity at the Kyle place in Indian Springs, Georgia. The year was 1975, and the smell of spring flowers was all around. It was a joyous day, and the Mullins were expecting their second child. While sitting at the breakfast table and preparing to head off for work, Jose called out to Mullins. "Come quick; I think it's time," she says in a mild voice. "Time for what?" Mullins replies as he continues his morning coffee. Then suddenly, Jose screams, "The baby's coming!" Three-year-old Levi watched in confusion as his mother struggled to stand.

Suddenly realizing what she'd just said, Mullins jumped up from the table, grabbed the car keys, and ran out the door. When he got to the car, he realized that he'd left Jose and three-year-old Levi in the house. So he runs back into the house, where Jose is angry enough to bite his head. "Come on, honey," says Mullins. "What about Levi and my emergency bag" she replied. But, of course, this was not in Mullin's plans for today. But finally, he grabbed his son and the emergency bag and headed to the hospital emergency room. When he arrived at the emergency entrance, he parked the car, ran inside, and told the ER desk clerk, "I'm having a baby." The clerk looked at Mullins and shook her head. "The crazy ward is that way, sir," she said. "Not me, my wife," Mullins shouted! By this time, Jose had gotten out of the car with 3-year-old Levi and was now standing right behind her husband. "Move Mullins, just move" she shouted! "Mam, I'm in labor and would appreciate some assistance, she said.

Finally, the ER team signed her in and took her back to wait for the doctor. Meanwhile, Mullins remembered that Levi didn't get to finish breakfast at home, so they headed to the cafeteria. There he meets Dr. Summers, who is Jose's ob-gyn doctor. "Good morning, doctor. This is my son Levi" says Mullins. "Wow, he has grown so much," the doctor replied. "So, how's your oldest child doing these days?" Dr. Summers added. "What oldest child?" Mullins replied with a confused look on his face. "Come on, Dr. Summers, you know Levi was our firstborn," he added. "You mean you didn't know?" she replied. "Didn't know what?" says Officer Mullins. "Mr. Mullins, I delivered Levi three years ago, and he was not the firstborn. Did your wife not tell you that she'd given birth before" she asked with a confused look.

Officer Mullins was stunned by what he'd just heard. He was in a state of shock. There was no way that this beautiful, loving wife would keep something like this from him. Their marriage was built on trust. "Oh my God in heaven," Mullins whispered to himself as tears began to well in his eyes. He knew what old man Kyle had done. He walked away and suddenly turned around and asked: "How long ago?" "Well, I can't be certain about the exact date, but this is something that you should discuss with your wife. I'm sure there's an explanation. Now, if you will excuse me, I believe I have another baby boy to deliver," she said as she hurried to the delivery room. In shock, Mullins searched his heart for answers and wondered if there were more childhood secrets. He was at a loss for words. He began to wonder about Jose's childhood and the events that took place while she was held captive by her father, Mr. Kyle. From the time he found her chained in that old wooden shack behind the bowling alley until now, he'd never questioned her past. He promised to protect and love her no matter what. And now he had a choice to make. First, he turned to his son Levi and told him how much he loved him. Then three-year-old Levi asked, "Daddy, why are you crying?" "I'm crying because I'm happy, son," Mullins replied.

After waiting for hours, Dr. Summers finally came out and told Mullins that he was the proud father of another baby boy. He shook the doctor's hand and thanked her for everything. "There's just one more thing, Mr. Mullins," said Dr. Summers. "Your wife has given birth to two children in the past three years, which can be quite stressful for any woman. Especially a woman in her early forty's." "I understand," he replied as he struggled to hold back the tears. Mullins and his son entered the room to find his wife holding a beautiful baby boy. He leaned over and gave her a gentle kiss. "I love you, Mrs. Mullins," he said. And I love you, Mr. Mullins, she replies. "Okay, son, come over and say hello to your little brother." He looked at Jose, and she was crying. "Why the tears, honey?" "It's nothing," she answered. But what Mullins didn't know was that each time she gave birth, it brought back memories of the baby girl she once held in her arms. A time when she was a young girl locked away and isolated from the loving arms of her mother. She would remember when she was given a toy doll by her father, Mr. Kyle, and told to shut up the whining. Jose would never forget the long days and nights waiting for Mr. Kyle to bring her baby girl back to her. But it never happened. Whenever she found out she was expecting, she would pray to God for a baby girl. But once again, it was another baby boy.

Two days passed, and it was time for Mullins to take his beautiful wife and son home. He brought flowers, and his son Levi got chocolate candy. "Oh my goodness. Thanks, guys," Jose said as she hugged Levi. "Where's mine?" Mullins asked. "You've had more than enough big guy," she replied jokingly. As they were about to leave, Dr. Summers came into the room. "Okay, guys, take care of this little man, and Mr. Mullins, you take care of this beautiful wife of yours," she added. "I promise to do exactly as the doctor has ordered. Now may I take my lovely wife home?" "Yes, you may, sir," says Dr. Summers. When they all got into the car, Mullins looked over at Jose and told her that nothing was as important as she and the children. "You make it sound like you're going away or something," says Jose. Mullins briefly gazed into her eyes and leaned over for a gentle kiss before turning his attention to his newborn. "Okay, let's go home, champ," he said.

When Jose walked through the door, she was surprised that Mullins had cleaned the house. It was so neat that she asked, "Okay, Mr. Mullins, where's the maid? Because I know you didn't do this." "Oh yes, I did," he replied jokingly. They had fun laughing and enjoying their new baby boy for the day. But at bedtime, Jose's sadness surfaced again as her eyes started to well with tears. This time was different, and it didn't seem she could shake the memories of the daughter taken from her thirty years earlier. At first, the nightmares were every other night. Then they began to come every night with such intensity that it woke her. One night she started talking in her sleep, repeatedly saying, "Give me my baby" until Mullins woke her up. "What's wrong, baby? It's just a dream," he said. As he held her close, he realized she was shaking as if she were cold. "Should I call the doctor?" he asked. "No, I'm fine; let's just try and get some sleep," she said.

As Mullins lay in bed with his arms firmly around Jose's shoulders, he couldn't help but think about what Dr. Summers had told him about early childbirth. This would be something that Mullins would have to deal with in the future. But he was hopeful that it would be at her request rather than his own. There was never any question concerning whether he would forgive her for not telling him. His only concern was if she could forgive herself for not telling him the truth initially. After all, Jose was only 15 years old when she gave birth to her first child. Old man Kyle kept it a secret by confiding in the same doctor he had used years earlier when Jose's mother, Josephine, gave birth in that old wooden shack. It seemed that Dr. Lewis didn't care what old man Kyle did as long as it was done to a person of color.

When Jose awakened the following day, she found breakfast on the nightstand with a note from her husband. It read, "Love you so much." She started crying as she read the letter, then suddenly, clinching it in her hands, she held it close to her heart. How would she ever find the words to say to the man who rescued her from the Kyles and took her as his wife? To have and to hold, to love and to cherish, to honor and obey for as long as they both shall live. What could she do to fix her marriage? But, in her heart, she knew that honesty was the only way. So she decided to tell him the whole truth as soon as he returned from the supermarket. She knew he wouldn't be gone long because he had taken the week off to help her with the kids.

Finally, Mullins returned to the kitchen to put away the groceries. Afterward, he entered the bedroom and sat on the bed next to Jose. She looked at him and said, "I have a confession to make." Mullins replied, "Not now." Then he leaned over and kissed her on her forehead. "You and the kids are my life; everything I am is because of you." He explained how blessed they were to have a relationship built on trust. "I just want you to know that nothing in the world could make me stop loving you," he added. "Now, what did you have to tell me that was so important?" José found herself speechless. After hearing her husband pour out his heart, she couldn't find the words to say. She knew what she wanted to say, but she could not say it. Mullins could see that she was afraid, so he told her to hold the thought. It would be harder for her to tell him about her past, especially after he told her their lives were built on trust. He then turned his attention to his newborn son. "How's my little man today," he said. "Don't you think it's about time we start calling him by his name?" Jose asked jokingly.

Suddenly Mullins realized that he had been so concerned with what Dr. Summers had told him about his wife's medical history that he didn't even ask for his son's name. Jose looked at him and smiled. "His name is Robert Mullins II," she said. "So you named him after me?" I can't believe you named him after me. See, that's why I love you so much," he added. "It was the least I could do since it was the last one," Jose replied. "So I guess we'll call him Bobby if that's okay with you," Mullins said jokingly. "That's fine with me," said replied. He was one proud father who couldn't wait to tell the fellows at work that he had a son named after him.

Now three-year-old Levi is awake and ready to have fun with his newborn brother. "What's his name," asked Levi. "Come over here," says Mullins. His name is Robert, but we'll call him Bobby. Is that ok with you" he asked. In response, Levi yelled, Bobby! As Jose watched them play with little Bobby, her mind was spinning in high gear. She was trying to figure out a way to tell her husband about her past without losing the perfect family they had built over the past four years. They had formed an unbreakable bond. While sitting there in bed and watching her husband play with their two boys, she couldn't help but think of the good times they'd shared.

Things like going to the movies for the first time at age forty. Or the first time she went into a restaurant. Jose even remembered as far back as the beginning when Mullins brought her to his small one-bedroom apartment and gave her his bed while he took the couch. She remembered cooking him breakfast the following day and giving him his first passionate kiss. But most of all, she thought about how he made her feel safe. Thoughts like these made it even more difficult for Jose to confess her past.

And now it was time to put the kids to bed after a long, fun-filled day with Dad. It was also a time that Jose dreaded because of her bad dreams about her long-lost baby girl. It was mental torture that seemed never to end. But tonight, Mullins was ready to answer the bell. He had decided to get to the root cause of her nightmares. It was around midnight, and Jose was sound asleep. Mullins finally fell asleep as well, and then it happened. Jose sat on the bed and started screaming, "Please don't take my baby." Mullins reached for her, and she began fighting him off. "Jose wake up; it's me, baby," shouted Mullins. Finally, she was awake and started to cry. "I just can't do it anymore," she said. "Can't do what, baby? Talk to me, Jose," he says.

The time had come when Jose had no choice but to tell her husband of her horrible past. So she tells Mullins, "I have a confession about my childhood at the Kyle place, and I am so afraid that I'm going to lose you and the kids." With tears in her eyes, she started begging, "Please don't leave me now." Mullins looked into her eyes, gently placing his hand over her lips. He began telling her everything she wanted to say to him. He could see how painful it was for her to say the words, so he decided to display them. "I already know what old man Kyle did to you, and I know he took your child." Jose listened with teary eyes as she watched her husband struggle to make sense of her reasons for keeping the secret. Mullins then removed his fingers from Jose's lips and told her that she didn't have to say a word. "I feel so dirty right now, says Jose. But the one thing that I know for sure is that this dirty secret has to come out." "It has to come out now because it's choking the life out of everything I am." When I was a young teen, maybe, 14 years old, this mean and evil old man who held me captive did horrible things to me. He hurt me badly almost every night. And on the weekends, when he was all liquored up, he would come into my tiny room and hurt me for hours. I begged him to stop, but instead, he beat me. He beat me so much that I became afraid of him. A few months later, my stomach swelled, and I had no idea why.

Then finally, I felt these horrible pains and began to scream out loud. That's when Mrs. Kyle came into my room and told me to shut up. Usually, she would only visit me at Christmas. First, she would walk into the room and stare at me for a moment. Then she would throw me a toy of some sort. And then, without saying a word, turn and left the room as if she hated me. But she was angry at me this time because of my swollen belly. "What in the hell have you done now," she asked her husband. "Go on and get out of here. I'll take care of the girl. Go on now, git," old man Kyle said.

"That's when Mr. Kyle went for the doctor. His name was Dr. Lewis. The pain was so bad that I could hardly feel my legs", Jose said. The doctor told me to push harder, and finally, after several attempts, it was finished, and the baby started to cry. I looked to see what it was and asked if I could hold it. The doctor gave me the baby, and I saw it was a beautiful baby girl. She was even prettier than the dolls he'd given me at Christmas. I wanted to keep her, but Mr. Kyle took her and told me he had to clean her up. He said yes when I asked if he would bring her back to me. But after the doctor finished my bath and helped me put on clean clothing, they left the room, and I never saw my baby girl again. Mr. Kyle continued to bring me food and water for the next few days, but he never returned with my baby girl. Finally, he told me to stop whining and play with the dolls. I knew then that she was gone forever. Over the years, I tried very hard to forget, but since I've been with you, I have thought about my baby girl and where she might be each time I've given birth to a child.

The thing I remember most about the time of her birth is when I went out back. The leaves on the trees were turning colors and falling to the ground. "Every year, I would chase the falling leaves for fun," Jose said. "Then I would pretend that my baby girl was falling in my arms." Mullins listened with teary eyes as his wife placed her heart in his hands. It was the most horrific confession he'd ever heard. And to listen to these words coming from the woman that he loved was heartbreaking. Mullins had to find a way to bring closure to Jose's devastating past that could not be undone. Her long-lost baby girl was also her baby sister.

And now, after hearing the entire story of Jose's horrible past, Mullins could only hold her in his arms as tight as he could and make her feel safe. He could feel her whole body tremble as she wept in his arms. "I will do everything in my power to find your daughter," Mullins promised. He knew in his heart that the chance of finding the child his wife had given birth to over thirty years earlier was almost impossible. However, he would leave no stone unturned if there was any chance. The next day, while sitting at the GBI police station, Officer Mullins began to stare at the Missing person wall. He thought to himself, what if there was an adoption record of some sort that would lead to the whereabouts of Jose's daughter? Then suddenly, an idea came to mind.

Officer Mullins left for the local adoption agency in Jackson, Georgia. The adoption agency was a family-owned business in the Browning family for years. When he arrived, the desk clerk, Sarah Jenkins, asked if she could help. "Good morning, mam; my name is Officer Robert Mullins. I'm working on an old adoption case with the GBI in Fulton County. So if it's alright with you, I'd like to check some of your adoption records," he said. "How far back are we talking?" she asked. "Well, I might be looking back as far as 1946," Mullins replied. "That would be over thirty years ago. So you got a name," Sarah asked. "No, I don't, but I was hoping to just browse through some old records, so if you don't mind pointing me in that direction, I'd like to get started," he replied. She got up from her desk and showed Officer Mullins the older adoption records. "These are the older records over here," she said. "I try to keep them in order, but they're always getting mixed up. I get so mad because the other girl that works here is so messy." "Oh my goodness. I'm just talking and talking. But don't you pay me no attention and let me know if I can help you," she said as she winked at Mullins. "I will call you if I need you," Mullins responded.

As he began looking through the adoption records, Mrs. Jenkins called someone and told them that a black policeman was going through old adoption records. "I think he's with the GBI in Atlanta. I'll call you back when he leaves," she said, in a whisper, before quickly hanging up the phone. After watching for a few minutes, Mrs. Jenkins got up and went to the records area and asked if he'd found anything of interest. Officer Mullins told her that it was an official police business and showed her his badge. "Well, excuse me," she said as she turned and returned to her desk. Mullins just shook his head. "This woman is about to get on my nerves," he said in a shallow voice.

After a couple of hours, Mullins finally found an adoption record that matched the same month for Jose's little girl. And the donor was none other than Mr. Kyle of Indian Springs, Georgia. The child was adopted by a local couple on the 5th of October in 1946 when she was only eight weeks old. That meant the child was born in August of 1946. At the same time that Jose remembers having her child. She was never sure of the actual date because she didn't have a calendar and couldn't read or write. But she mentioned to Mullins the night before that the leaves on the trees were turning colors and her memories of chasing the falling leaves for fun. So the birth of Jose's child would have been around August or the fall season. Unfortunately, the name of the couple who adopted the child was not listed. The only mention of custody was to the owners of the agency. But there was another transfer of custody document in the files. The agency owners, Michael and JoAnn Browning did not maintain custody of the child. So who were the final adoptive parents? Officer Mullins put the file back in the cabinet drawer and left. "Thanks for the help," he said as he went to the agency. "Hope you found what you needed," Sarah replied.

When Mullins left, Mrs. Jenkins went to the records area to see what he had found. She had watched him close enough to observe the last file drawer; he searched and opened the drawer and found that the Browning file had been disturbed. When Sarah opened the file and noticed page 2 was missing. She immediately called Mr. Browning, the owner of the Browning Hardware & Gun Shop.

"Good morning Mr. Browning; this is Sarah at the adoption agency. "How's Mrs. JoAnn doing these days?" "She's just fine, Sarah. How can I help you" he asked. "I'm calling to let you know that a policeman out of Atlanta just left here, and he was searching for adoption records from 1946. I think you should come by and check your files," she said. "I'll be right over," he replied. And don't let anyone else go through those records without a warrant. That's a private business, and I commit to my clients to keep matters confidential.

Mr. Browning knew that trouble was on the horizon. "JoAnn comes in here; we got problems. It's that black cop again," he said. "What black cop, hon?" she asked. "The same cop that worked on the Kyle case, and he just left the agency, putting his nose in our files," he added. "Oh my God, which files was he looking for?" she asked. "He was looking for a 1946 file, which could only mean one thing. That damn woman he found chained up at the Kyle place has finally started talking," he said. "I told you that we should've never got involved with old man Kyle" JoAnn replied. "What if he finds out who she is, and even worse, what if he finds out who her husband is?" she added. "Well, he didn't find out from the file because it's not there," said Mr. Browning. "But he knows that we know, and he's a cop, so you damn well better fix this, Michael," JoAnn says. Lock the front door, and let's go to the agency. We're closed for the day," he said.

Meanwhile, Mullins is going to the Butts County courthouse to see if a birth certificate is available. He's hoping to find the parents' names if there is any such record. However, he knows this is a long shot, considering the secrecy of the birth and adoption. He must also decide whether to tell Jose that he found a file. It might push her over the edge mentally, and that's not exactly what the doctor ordered. When Officer Mullins arrived at the Butts County courthouse, he went into the Office of Public Records. "Morning, Ladies," he said. "Well, good morning to you, sir. What can we help you with today" the clerk asked. "I'm trying to find a birth certificate for a missing person, and I was hoping you could check the county records for a child born around August of 1946." "Well, let me just take a look," she said. After searching the records for a few minutes, she finally found the files for August 1946. "Here we are, sir. There were about 14 babies in August 1946. Which one are you looking for?" "Well, do you have one associated with a Mr. Kyle of Indian Springs?" Mullins asked. "Let me see here. Okay, I think I've found it", she paused. "This is strange," she says. "What's so strange about it" Mullins replies. Well, it shows Kyle as the father, but the information on the mother is left blank." "Now, it does say here that it was a seven-pound baby girl. I have never seen one like this before", she added. Can I have a copy of that says, Officer Mullins?

"I don't see why not, but I'll have to charge you for the certified copy," she said. "That will be fine," Mullins replied. He was no closer to discovering who and where this Jane Doe child was because his name was not on the birth certificate. She had listed her as a Jane Doe. There was no way that Officer Mullins could tell his wife what he'd found. At least not until he had some solid leads to her possible whereabouts. This type of information could cause her to suffer a mental breakdown. And he remembered all too well what Jose had gone through right after she was found chained up in that horrible wooden shack at the Kyle place. He knew that Michael and JoAnn Browning were his only genuine leads. But he also knew that they would never volunteer the information. Mullins decided to take another look at the certificate, hoping that there was something that he had missed. He noticed that Michael Browning signed the doctor's signature. And Jose was confident that a man named Dr. Lewis had delivered her child. Since Mr. Kyle and Dr. Lewis were deceased, the only persons left to ask were the Brownings.

The Brownings finally arrived at the adoption agency, and Michael Browning asked Sarah to describe the officer that came in to check the records. When she told the officer, they both knew it was, in fact, Officer Mullins. "Dammit, that cop is putting his nose in something he has no business messing with," he says to his wife, JoAnn. "One thing for sure, he knows who we are, and he'll be back," she said. "And dammit, we'll be ready when he does," Michael responded angrily.

Michael Browning went to his office in the rear of the adoption agency and unlocked his desk drawer. Inside the drawer was a small book with names and phone numbers. He dialed a number, and a woman answered. He asked to speak to her husband. When her husband answered the phone, Michael said, "This is Michael Browning, and we need to talk." "First of all, I haven't heard from you in thirty years, but what can I do for you," the man says. "There's the trouble with your daughter's adoption. That damn cop, Officer Mullins, has found out that his wife had a child in 1946, and he's digging through all sorts of records," Michael says. "He has to be stopped before he gets any closer," he added. "Okay, I'll make some calls and see if I can't get him to back off," the man said as he continued smoking his cigar. Whoever this man was, it was sure that he didn't want anyone to know that his adopted daughter had a black mother. And more importantly, he didn't want his daughter to know. But who was this man that adopted Jose's child thirty years ago, and where did he live?

When Mullins got back to his office, the captain called him in. "Where the heck you been all morning Mullins?" Captain Mack asked. "I went to Jackson, Georgia, to take care of some family business. Is that a problem, Captain" he asked jokingly. "It's not a problem, detective, but remember that you only have two more years before retirement. So let sleeping dogs lie, for crying out loud," Captain Mack replies. "What's going on, Captain," he asked. "Well, it seems that you're making some people very nervous. I don't know what it is, but I know that they're compelling, and you better back off before they make trouble for all of us," he added. Mullins suddenly realized the Captain was serious. This was a game-changer for sure. He knew someone connected to the Browning Adoption Agency had informed Captain Mack of his recent visit. Mullins knew this could mean trouble at the station because he didn't know all the players. That evening when he got home from work, Jose was waiting on pins and needles. She couldn't wait to hear what he had discovered about her long-lost daughter. Finally, he entered the door, and Jose was standing and waiting as if it were her birthday. He looked her in the eyes and, with deep regret, lied to her for the first time because he didn't know what effect the information might have on her mental state. Mullins loved his wife so much, and the thought of being dishonest with her caused his eyes to well with tears. "What's wrong, Robert, and why the tears," Jose asked. "Nothing's wrong. I wish I could do more," he answered as he kissed her forehead.

The next day when Mullins arrived at the station, he had received a voicemail from Michael Browning. He asked Officer Mullins to please give him a call. Mullins looked up, and the Captain stared directly at him through the glass window. It was as if he already knew what the voicemail was about. Mullins immediately got up from his desk and went into Captain Mack's office. "I saw you were watching me through your office window, Captain, and you've always been a straight shooter. So what's going on" Mullins asked. "Com' on Mullins, you're digging through this guy's records. What do you expect him to do" Captain Mack replied. "I can't explain it right now, Captain, but if you give me a little more time, it'll all come to light. Just give me more time, and I promise I'll stay in bounds," Mullins said. "You damn well better stay the hell away from that adoption agency," said Captain Mack. "And that's an order," he added. "I can't promise you that, Captain," Mullins shouted. "I'm not asking you for a damn promise. I gave you a direct order to stay away," the Captain responded angrily. "Don't make me do it, Mullins. Because I will sit your ass behind a desk for the next two years," he added.

Officer Mullins turned away and walked out of the office. He knew that time was running out, so he decided not to call Michael Browning back but to visit him. This time he used an official vehicle for the trip to Butts County in case the county police decided to try and stop him on a road violation. Mullins knew most of the police tricks and knew they would find a reason if they wanted to stop you. When he got to Jackson, he parked on the town square, right in front of Browning's Hardware and

Gun Shop. He walked inside, and there he saw Mrs. Browning. "What can I help you with," JoAnn Browning asked. "I'm looking for a Michael Browning, mam," Mullins answered. "Hold on a second; he's in the back. And who should I say is here to see him" she asked. "You can tell him that Officer Mullins is here, mam," he replied. She stopped immediately and turned to take another look. "Is everything alright, mam?" he asked. "Just wait here," she responded with a frightened look. When she left the storefront, she hurried to her husband's office in the rear and closed the door. "He's here, Michael. He's here inside our store. What are we going to do" she asked. "First thing we're going to do is just calm down while I go out here and see what Mr. Detective wants," Michael said. He walks from the back of the store to meet with Officer Mullins. "Howdy, sir, what can I do for you today," he asks. "Well, I received your voicemail when I got to the office this morning, and I decided just to drop in and pay you a visit," says Mullins. "So, you're the infamous Officer Mullins who broke the Kyle case about five years ago," he says. "If you want to call it that," Mullins replied.

"Well, I just wanted to remind you that the case was closed, and when old man Kyle was killed, the case died with him," Mr. Browning said. "And, if you ever go into my files and poke your nose where it doesn't belong, I'll have your badge, mister, and you can count on it," he added. "You listen to me, you all mighty bastard," says Officer Mullins. "That woman I found chained like an animal on the Kyle property is my wife. And if you ever refer to her as a closed case, you won't have to look very far for my badge 'cause I'll shove it up your ass," he added as he turned and walked to the door. "And while you're counting, count on that, Mr. Browning," he said.

When Mullins left the town square, he noticed a county patrol car following him, so he pulled over. The county patrol car pulled beside him and asked if he was having trouble. Officer Mullins got out of his car and showed the deputy his badge. "Do you know what this is, a deputy?" Mullins asked. "Yes sir, I do," he said. "Then understand this, I don't know who told you to follow me, but I have jurisdiction all over Georgia. Can you remember that deputy" he asked. "Yes, I can, detective," he replied. "You have a good day," said Mullins as he returned to his patrol car and left the county. While driving, he watched in his rearview mirror as the county deputy turned off. He knew everything was connected to his search for the birth documents of Jose's daughter.

When he got home from work, Jose was hoping that he would say, "I've found your baby girl. But she knew it would be difficult. She also knew how hard this could be, not only on Mullins but on her entire family. When Mullins got home, Jose sat in the kitchen with her two sons, Levi and Bobby. "Okay, superwoman. What are you doing out of bed" Mullins asked. "And give me my Lil man Mullins Jr," he added. "First of all, your little man is sleeping, and I had the hardest time getting him to fall asleep. So don't wake him," Jose says as Mullins takes little Bobby from her lap.

Meanwhile, he continued to talk about everything except the issue of his wife's long-lost baby girl. Finally, she asks, "Did you find anything new today?" "Mullins turns to his wife and reluctantly tells her, "There's nothing new," and heads to the shower to avoid further conversation. Really? says Jose in a whisper. She went to the oven to turn the golden fried chicken before turning her attention back to her hungry husband, who was headed straight for the shower. Jose knew her husband well enough that something was wrong if he came in from work and bypassed freshly fried chicken. But eager as she was for answers, she was careful not to pressure him just yet.

Chapter 5: Return of Racial Threats

Later that night, Jose began to toss and turn in her sleep. Finally, she started saying, "Let me go, let me out." Mullins noticed that she was sweating to the point that her pillow was wet. "Wake up, Jose," he whispered. When she awakened, her eyes welled with tears. All he could do was hold her in his arms. He knew she didn't need to be alone, especially with two small kids. He was reminded of the instructions from the Learning Center when Jose first recovered from Kyle's place, so he decided to take some time off work. They told him that she could relapse and lose awareness if exposed to certain things from her past. But Mullins knew in his heart that Jose had become this strong person. He knew her inner strength was her awareness of history and her determination never to look back. Jose refused to mourn for her child because when you grieve for the loss of a child, you've accepted that the child is gone forever. And despite everything, she never lost faith that she would see her child again one day.

The following day when Mullins awakened, he found that Jose had made breakfast. "This is a pleasant surprise," said Mullins. "I thought we could have a nice breakfast before the boys awake," Jose replies. "Sounds good to me," says Mullins as he sits at the kitchen table. They talked for a while before Mullins said, "I have to go to work, but I'll be home early. I'm also taking some time off to help you out around here with little ones." "That would be so nice," Jose replies. "But I'm okay here," she added. "It's already decided," he said.

Mullins got up and went to the office. He sat there for about an hour before the Captain came out and called him into his office. "What's up, Captain," says Mullins. "How's that wife and that new baby of yours doing these days," he asked. "Well, I wanted to talk to you about some much-needed time off," Mullins replied. "Say no more," said Captain Mack. "Take as much time as you need," he added. "Okay, Sir, thanks," he replied. When he left the Captain's office, he thought to himself. "Damn, that was way too easy." But he gathered his briefcase and went anyway. As soon as he drove off, Captain Mack called the same gentleman smoking the cigar. When the man answered the phone, Captain Mack told him that Officer Mullins had just taken a leave of absence. "Let's just hope he minds his damn business," the man responded as he angrily smashed his cigar in the ashtray. "He damn well better," Captain Mack replied.

When Mullins got home, Jose was surprised to see him back so early. "So I see you decided not to stay," she said. "No, I just missed my wife so much that I couldn't stay," Mullins replied.

"Seems Captain Mack was all too eager to give me some time off," he added. They sat in the kitchen and made small talk for a while but beating around the bush wasn't going to fly with Jose. She knew something was bothering Mullins. "Okay, Officer Robert Mullins, I need you to hear me," says Jose as she pulls her chair face to face with her husband. "When a woman loves a man, she knows that man. She knows him in ways he doesn't know himself because she pays attention to her man. Not only to what he says but more importantly to what he doesn't say." "And right now, every fiber in my body tells me that you're onto something, and you're not telling me, so start talking, Mister." Jose leaned back and folded her arms, hoping her analysis would ignite conversation. "So you're giving me the old "mac daddy" fold the arms thing, huh," Mullins said jokingly as he tried to play it off. However, he was pretty surprised that she could dissect his male egotistical habits with such accuracy. But being a man, he did what most men do. He developed a case of amnesia. "I don't know what you're talking about," he says. But this time, Jose wasn't in the mood for games. Suddenly, she became emotional and walked out on the balcony to try and hide her tears. Mullins went out after her and found her crying uncontrollably. The time had come for Jose to unleash her anger. "I have been caged like an animal from the time I was a child. I was beaten and raped by my father so many times I couldn't count them all. My flesh and blood was ripped from my arms the same way I was taken from my mother. I cried day and night until my eyes ran dry, begging for my child's return. So I will not apologize for wanting to hold her again, for wanting to know if she's alive and well. To touch her flesh and feel the blood running warm in her veins would give me so much joy. So if I sound a little angry, you have to excuse me because I'd like to reach down into the pits of hell and choke the truth out of old man Kyle."

Mullins was lost for words as he listened to his wife with a careful ear. She had just released all the anger trapped inside for the last thirty years. The anger that smothers the beacon of light that gives hope to the brokenhearted when all else has failed. There was no way Jose was letting go of this opportunity to hold her child again finally. And Mullins knew that she was both determined and prepared to go the distance. But he also knew that this fight could be dangerous not only for Jose but for his two sons as well.

"Okay, Jose, says Mullins, I'll go back to Jackson tomorrow and talk to some people who might be able to give us some answers." "But I make no promises except to do my best," he adds. "That's all I would ever ask of you," Jose replied as she wiped her eyes. Mullins sat up most of the night trying to figure out an angle of approach that didn't involve contact with Michael and JoAnn Browning. They were the only leads he had so far, and there wasn't a chance they would volunteer any information leading to the whereabouts of Jose's daughter. He couldn't put his finger on it, but he knew that Captain Mack had been contacted by someone who wanted him to back off. It crossed his mind to ask the Captain. They had always had a relationship based on trust. But was that confidence strong enough to take a chance on his family's safety? Mullins would have to tell him the whole story, which would put Jose at risk. There were so many unanswered questions. Does the Captain already know? Is the Captain involved in keeping the adoption a secret? Even worse, is Captain Mack protecting someone who may have harmed the child? That was the main reason that Mullins didn't want Jose involved.

He didn't want to chance a mental relapse if it turned out her baby girl didn't live past the eight weeks at the adoption agency. However, it seemed more likely that she was alive because of the efforts to keep it a secret.

The phone rings and Jose gets excited because she thinks Mullins has some good news. She answers the phone, but it's not her husband. Instead, there's a stranger on the phone saying nothing. So Jose hangs up the phone and goes over to attend to little Bobby. But the phone rings again, and she wonders if she should answer it. She decides to answer, and the person on the phone starts to breathe heavily but doesn't speak. "Hello, who's there," Jose asks. "Okay, If you don't want to talk, then don't call," she says before she hangs up the phone. When she walks away, it rings again. Now Jose is concerned and decides this is the last time she will answer. "Stop calling me and leave me alone. Please," Jose pleads to the caller. But this time, it was Mullins who called. "Hold on baby. It's me, Robert. What's going on" he asks. "Someone keeps calling me and breathing hard on the phone," Jose said. "Okay, I'm on my way. The next time they call, don't hang it up. I'll try and trace the call when I get home," he said.

Then almost immediately, it rings again. This time she answered with the intent of just leaving it off the hook, just like her husband had instructed. Jose answered the phone and paused for a moment, trying to think if it were ok to speak. Then she spoke, "Hello may I help you," she asked. Surprisingly this time, the person answered and said: "Tell that nigger husband of yours he better back off and mind his business if he knows what's good for him." Jose was speechless. She laid the phone down as if it were a loaded weapon. She couldn't believe that after all these years, racism had resurfaced. Would the threatening phone calls trigger the mental relapse Mullins was warned about when Jose was released from the Learning Center? If nothing else, it was a reality check for Jose, and the only conclusion was that the search for her child might very well be a walk down memory lane. It was a time for a show of inner strength. A time when being strong was the only option that she had. She entered the boy's room and brought them together in her bedroom.

"Come on, Levi, get your toys. You can play in Mamma's room today," she said. "But Daddy said no toys in here," says Levi. "It's ok this time. I'll tell Daddy I did it," Jose responds. She kept looking at the clock because it seemed like an eternity, although it had only been twenty minutes. Then a few minutes later, Mullins arrived. He had asked his partner, Dave, to meet him at the house and to bring the phone tracer. So they hooked the tracer to find it had been cleared. The caller knew how long to stay on the phone to avoid being traced.

Thanks, man, I appreciate you coming out," said Mullins as he glanced at his frightened wife. "Tell you what, Robert, why don't you keep this unit with you and bring it back when you return to the office? It's signed out to me, and I'll cover you," said Dave.

"And listen, if you want help, tell me what's happening. Maybe I can help," said Dave. "Nah, I've got it, but if I need you, I'll call you," he added as he walked Dave to the door.

When Dave left, Mullins turned his attention immediately to his wife, Jose. "Are you going to be able to hang in there," he asked. "I told you it could get worse before it gets better." Jose just sat in silence for several minutes. Finally, Mullins realized she wasn't responding to his comments. He called out to her, "Jose," but she still didn't respond. Mullins went over to where Jose was sitting and began to shake her, calling out her name, trying to get her to snap out of the silent mode. Then suddenly, she snaps back as if she'd been awakened from a deep sleep. "I'm ok," says Jose. "For the first time in my life, I felt close to my baby girl. And when I heard that mysterious voice on the phone, I felt a connection to my child." Mullins thought for a minute that he had lost Jose, once again, to a world of silence and fear. She had the same look in her eyes when she testified in court against old man Kyle. He was reminded of those powerful words in the courtroom on the day that she referred to her father, Mr. Kyle, as an evil person. "Right there," she said, with a trembling voice, pointing her finger at her father. Those words would forever echo in his ear.

The following day Mullins decided to visit the Learning Center and talk with Dr. Tonya Price, Jose's attending physician. When he left his driveway, he noticed a white van parked on the street across from his house. His detective instincts kicked into high gear when he saw the van was following him. They followed him to the Learning Center. Mullins got out of his car and glanced briefly at the van. Before entering the building, he made a mental note of two white male occupants. The guys in the van wondered what he was doing there. "What in the hell is he doing here," said the van driver. "I don't know. Maybe we should call Boss," the passenger replied.

Interestingly enough, Boss was the same man Mr. Browning and Captain Mack had spoken with on the phone. This meant that whoever Boss was, he was the adoptive parent of Jose's daughter. And he would protect this well-kept secret at all costs.

Meanwhile, Mullins ran into Dr. Price inside the Learning Center. "Well, hello there, Officer Mullins," she said. "And greetings to you, doctor," he replied. "I was hoping to talk with you about my wife, Jose," he added. "Is she alright, and why didn't you bring her with you?" she asked. "Well, it's complicated," said Mullins. "Complicated," she asked. "Now you have my attention Officer Mullins so tell me exactly what's going on." "Well, I just found out recently that Jose had a child when she was 15 years old," he said. "And how did you find out," she asked. "Does it matter?" Mullins replied. "Yes, it matters a great deal because this is the type of thing that could trigger a mental relapse, and that won't be a pretty picture," she says angrily. "Oh, my God. How long have you known about this" he asked. She paused for a moment. Officer Mullins asked again. "How long, Dr. Price?" Finally, she answered. "I've known all along, and if you dig deeper, you had better make sure you find what she's looking for, or else" she added. "Or else what," said Mullins. "Or else you may lose her forever," she shouted. Mullins was saddened by what he'd just heard. "Thank you, Doctor," Officer Mullins left her office with his head down in sorrow and sadness. Dr. Price was seriously concerned for Jose, considering all she'd been through at Kyle's residence. She knew that giving birth would always be problematic for Jose with the possibility of permanent memory loss. It could be traumatic for the Mullins family.

Mullins left the Learning Center with a different attitude. He was now on a mission. It was either to find the daughter or lose Jose. And losing Jose was not an option. Tears welled in his eyes as he began thinking of what would become of his sons, Levi and little Bobby, if anything ever happened to their mother. When he walked into the parking lot, his first thought was to go to the white van and confront the two guys. But he knew they would never give him the name of the person who sent them, so he left the parking lot, and the van continued to follow. "That's right, fellows, keep following," Mullins mumbled. He led them to Jackson and parked right in front of Browning's Hardware & Gun Shop. He had decided that the only way to dig deeper was to open the can of worms. So he went inside the store and asked for Michael Browning. "Mr. Browning isn't here," said JoAnn. Before Mullins could respond, Michael Browning walked in from the rear of the store.

"Okay, Officer Mullins, what do you want now," Michael asked. The same thing I wanted before, and I'll want it until I find it," Mullins responded. "So if you know the whereabouts of my wife's daughter, please tell us, and we won't cause any problems," he added. "It's more complicated than that, Officer Mullins.

Adoption records are kept private and personal for a reason," says Michael. "It's the law, and it's none of your business," he added. "Yes, it is the law, Mr. Browning. But when the adopted child has been taken from the mother, against her will, it becomes a crime, and that, sir, is my business," Mullins explained. "Just tell your wife that her daughter doesn't want to be found," JoAnn Browning said. Officer Mullins paused for a moment before responding. "Do you have children, Mrs. Browning?" he asked. "Yes, we have three children Mr. Mullins" she answered. "Then try to imagine what it would feel like to have one of those children ripped from your arms at birth," he said as he turned and left the store.

"Oh my God, Michael. He's not going to stop," JoAnn said. "Oh, he'll stop one way or the other little darling. One way or the other, and that's a promise," Michael responded as he walked to his office in the rear of the store to call the man called Boss. "Hey Boss, this nigger Mullins just paid me another visit, and frankly, I'm getting tired of seeing his damn face. "Oh, stop pissing in your pants, Michael; he's under tight watch," said Boss as he hung up the phone and smashed out his cigar in an ashtray. Now it seemed that Boss had seen about as much of Officer Mullins as he could stomach. So he called the Butts County Sheriff, who was his cousin. "Howdy Sheriff, I need a favor," said Boss. "You got it, cousin," Sheriff Wallace replied. "I need you to make this Officer Mullins fellow a little uncomfortable about coming to your town," Boss said. "I'll have one of the boys pull him over as he's leaving town," Sheriff Wallace replied. "And tell the wife we expect to see her at the Family Re-Union this year," he added.

When Mullins left for home, the white van continued to follow, but before he crossed the county line on Hwy 42, a Butts County patrol car cut in behind him. He didn't worry too much because he'd installed a recording device in his vehicle. And now the lights came on, and Officer Mullins pulled over to the side of the road. "Afternoon, officer," said Mullins. "Where you headed, boy," said the county deputy. "That's none of your business, deputy. Now, why did you stop me" asked Officer Mullins. "Get out of the car boy, said the deputy. "When Officer Mullins got out of the car, the deputy noticed he was wearing a firearm, so he quickly drew and aimed it at Officer Mullins. "What the hell are you doing wearing a gun, boy," the deputy asked. "Well, if you'd done your damn job and asked for my license and registration, then you would've known that I was a cop," said Officer Mullins.

At that time, Mullins pulled his jacket open to reveal the GBI badge on his waist belt. The deputy apologized for the mistake, but Officer Mullins told him he had it all recorded. "I'm kind of new on the force, and I need my job, so why don't we just pretend it never happened," the deputy said. "Why don't we talk about who gave the order to stop me, and then we might do some pretending," Officer Mullins added. "All I know is I got a call from the station to stop and apprehend this vehicle and to bring the occupant to the jail for questioning," the deputy said. "Did they tell you it was against the law to stop citizens for no reason?" Officer Mullins asked. "Come on, Officer Mullins, It's a small town, and I don't make the rules. So let's leave it at that," says the deputy. "That's the smartest thing you've said so far, but you tell whoever sent you that I don't scare easily."

The deputy got in his patrol car and turned back on Hwy 42 while the white van waited further down for Officer Mullins to pass. When he passed, the van continued to follow him. He knew they would soon lead him to someone connected to Jose's daughter, so he pretended not to notice them. But the white van didn't turn in behind him when he turned off at the pharmacy. That made him wonder what they were up to. So he entered the pharmacy and, while picking up some items for his newborn son, decided to call Jose to ensure he got everything. But when he reached home, there was no answer. He tried calling several times with no response. It was unusual so he became worried and hurried home. He looked for the white van along the way, but it was nowhere in sight. Now he began to wonder if the van was headed to his residence to frighten Jose and the kids. Mullins wondered if he should have confronted the stalkers from the beginning. He knew that if they were allowed to continue, it could have serious consequences. Especially if they ever came into direct contact with his family.

When Mullins arrived, Jose was cuddled in the bedroom with the kids. He could see that she was terrified for some reason. "What happened," Mullins asked. "They called me and said that they were coming for the kids and me," said Jose with a trembling voice. "They want our kids Robert. Why" she asked over and over. "Who wants the kids, Jose," Mullins asked. "They called me and told me to look out the window. And I saw two men standing and waving at me next to this White van," she explained as tears ran down her frightened face. "Then I told them my husband was home, and they said, "How could that be when we just saw him at the pharmacy." "How could they know Robert," said Jose as she held tight to his chest in fear. Mullins knew now that this awful thing of the past had found its way to his home. The place where his wife and kids should feel safe at all times. But now, the men in the white van had received instructions to target Jose. The game plan had changed, and Mullins knew it was only a matter of time before Jose would break down. He had to solve this case quickly, and quitting was not an option.

Mullins decided to call his partner Dave. "Dave, it's me, Mullins." "What's up, dude" Dave answered. "These bastards have brought this fight to my home. To my home Dave. The place where my wife and kids are supposed to feel safe," said Mullins. "I need to meet with you. But I need your word that I can trust you, " Mullins said. "Hell to the yeah, my man," Dave responds. "Okay, so I'll call you with the details tomorrow," he said. His partner Dave was a crazy white boy from Brooklyn, New York, who an elderly black woman raised. She adopted him when he was only seven years old after his parents were killed in a drive-by shooting. Dave always made it home for Thanksgiving with his seven brothers and four sisters. Of the twelve siblings were seven black males, two black females, and two white females. Of course, Dave was the only white male sibling who always got into trouble. Nevertheless, they loved each other dearly, even though they were all adopted. To sum it up, Dave was a serious but crazy white boy who didn't mind a good fight.

Meanwhile, Mullins was trying to comfort his wife and make her feel safe. "Let me clarify this to you, Jose," says Mullins. "No one is going ever to take our children away from us, and when I am finished with these bastards, they will regret the day they ever messed with my family," he added. Jose looked into his eyes and smiled because she knew in her heart that he would move heaven and hell for his family if he could. But Mullins had concluded that he could trust no one in that town. Not even his superior, Captain Mack, who connected to the man called Boss. The question remained, who and where was this man called Boss? Mullins knew that someone was controlling the Brownings and his Captain. And this was a question that had to be answered before he could find the path that led to the illegal adoption of Jose's daughter.

Finally, after Jose and the kids were settled down, Mullins decided to prepare dinner. While cutting up some vegetables, the phone rang. He answered the phone, and there was silence on the other end. "I don't know who you are, and frankly, I don't give a damn, but I will find you," he said. As he turned back into the kitchen, Jose was standing in the doorway. The phone call had awakened her. "Who was it," she asked. Mullins looked at her and said, "No one important." "And you, pretty lady, should be in bed," he added. But she knew he was worried and decided to stay and help with dinner. "Maybe you can use a second cook," Jose said jokingly. "I'd like that," Mullins replied. So they took advantage of the quiet time with the boys taking a nap. "Careful now, Mr.

Mullins," says Jose. "I know the doctor's orders," he replied as he held her close. Jose looked up at him and said: "I'm sorry for getting you and the kids mixed up in my past." Mullins quickly responded with a gentle kiss on her forehead. "There's nothing to be sorry for, and I admire a woman who's willing to go the distance for her child," he said.

After dinner, while getting ready for bed, Mullins glanced at his wife and told her that she was even more beautiful than the first time he laid eyes on her. He took the brush from her hand and began brushing her hair. Jose closed her eyes as he massaged her head with his fingers. Then, with her eyes closed, she whispered, "That feels so good." Afterward, she turned to her husband for a passionate kiss as they found their way to the bed, where they cuddled until the morning light. And then, of course, there was the sound of little Bobby, who was hungry or needing a diaper change. "It's your turn, honey," Mullins says to Jose. "Don't even try it, Mister," Jose replied. "Can't blame me for trying?" Mullins said as he rolled out of bed to change little Bobby.

Finally, it was time for Mullins to meet with his partner Dave to discuss his plans for finding out who was terrorizing his family. When he arrived at the waffle house in Locust Grove, his partner Dave was already there. "Damn, dude, you're late," he said jokingly. "Had a long and loving night with the wife. Something you'd know nothing about," Mullins replied. "Hey, I know a little something now," Dave replied. "Yeah, okay, but here's the plan," says Mullins

Everything I do at the station will be watched closely, so I'll need you to watch my back," he explained. Mullins went on to say, "Captain Mack is also involved." "What the hell are we talking about here, dude" Dave responded. "We're talking about a cover-up from something that happened years ago in 1946," Mullins replied. "What the heck does that have to do with you, man? Just spit it out," says Dave. "Okay, here goes, my wife was raped at age 14, and she gave birth to a baby girl. And that baby girl was taken away at birth and illegally adopted by someone in Jackson, Georgia. And now, after all these years, it's taken a toll on Jose, and she wants to find her," Mullins explained. "Wow, I'm gone need a minute to absorb this," Dave said.

"So what you're telling me is, we are looking for a kid that was taken over 30 years ago. Not to mention, she may not even want to be found," Dave added. "One more thing," says Mullins. The adoptive parents are doing everything they can to keep me from finding her. Someone with money and political power," he added. "Well, if it was illegal in 1946, then as far as I'm concerned, it's illegal now. What the hell? Count me in," says Dave. "So you're all in, right," asked Mullins. "Hell yeah, partner, let's do this," Dave replied.

And now the two GBI agents have agreed to challenge the political machine that could be the end of their careers. But together, they were intent on finding the stolen child. As far as Dave was concerned, corruption had always been something that he promised to fight. He promised that he'd to his adoptive mother because it was the reason behind the drive-by shooting that took the lives of his parents at an early age. She was the one who pushed little Dave to the ground and shielded him from the gunfire with her own body. And because the flying bullets didn't hit her, she gave him the nickname "Little Lucky." Even when she bought her lottery tickets, she would ask Dave for a number. But, of course, he didn't know what he was doing, nor did he know that she was playing the numbers. Until one Thanksgiving dinner, when all the siblings were at the dinner table, she confessed that she'd gotten most of her winning lottery numbers from Little Lucky Dave. They all laughed, except Dave, who was always the center of the family jokes. But the one thing that held this adopted family together was that it meant something when they gave their word. Their mother had always instilled in them the value of keeping your word. So this meant that Officer Mullins had a partner who would keep his word and do everything he could to help find Jose's daughter.

When they arrived back at the station, they ran into Captain Mack. "So let me guess. You love your job so much that you couldn't enjoy your vacation," Captain Mack says to Mullins. "Well, Captain, everything at home is fine, and the wife didn't want me around. So you're stuck with me," Officer Mullins replied as he and his partner Dave went to their respective desks. Captain Mack knew this could be trouble if Mullins continued digging away at the past in search of Jose's daughter. So he went into his office and closed the door and the blinds. When Dave noticed the blinds were shut, he snapped his finger at Mullins and pointed at the Captain's door. They both acknowledged that the Captain was concerned about Mullins coming back early off leave.

In the meantime, Captain Mack calls Boss. "Hey, he's back from vacation already. It seems that your accomplices pissed him off. "You listen to me carefully, Boss. Officer Mullins is not one to be bullied; if you continue down this road, he will pull the curtains down," says Captain Mack. "Well said, Captain. But I'm not afraid of some nigger GBI who wants to stick his nose in my damn business. We're talking about this daughter, and if you can't control your pit bull, then I will," Boss replied as he shut off his phone and threw it into the wall. It seemed that Boss was ready to take the fight to another level. But he was at least smart enough to call his hired accomplices in the white van and tell them to back off. He knew what needed to be done, so he left his home in Mobile, Alabama, and headed for Jackson, Georgia. Boss knew now that it would take something drastic to make this Mullins guy back off. So he called a guy who went by the name Lil Rick. This guy was an arms dealer who had done business with Browning's Hardware & Gun Shop. Boss asked Lil Rick to meet him at Browning's store in Jackson. When Lil Rick walked into the store, JoAnn Browning seemed shocked to see him because she knew it meant trouble for her family. "Why are you here, Rick," she asked. "Hey lady, just hold your horses because I didn't call this meeting," Lil Rick explained. "Wait here," she said as she left for the back office for her husband, Michael. When he came up front, he asked the same question as JoAnn. "Why are you here, Rick," he asked. About that time, Boss walked into the store. Michael immediately went to the entrance, turned on the closed sign, and locked the door. "Okay, is somebody ready to tell me what the hell is going on," says Michael.

"What in the hell does it look like" Boss shouted. "It looks like somebody can't control the niggers around here, and I'm gone have to do it my way," he said. "Now, you just wait a minute," says JoAnn. "Michael and I don't want any more dealings with you or your type," she added. "She's right Boss. We can't get involved with this mess because that nigger cop is a loose cannon," Michael explained. "Well, that's why I called Lil Rick to defuse the situation," says Boss. "And just how will he defuse a man who's dead set on bringing somebody to justice," JoAnn says. "And I hope you don't think we're providing any more guns for anything illegal," she added. "Of course not, and we don't intentionally hurt anyone as long as everybody minds their business," says Boss. "What we need to do is find a way to snatch away something that we can use to control this out-of-control cop," Boss added. He told Lil Rick to keep watch on Officer Mullin's wife, Jose. He wanted to know her schedule. Things like how often she leaves home, does she drive, and does she take the kids with her. "I know you're not thinking about hurting this woman or her children," says JoAnn. "I think this would be a good time for Mrs. Browning to exit the conversation, Michael," says Boss. "He's right, JoAnn," Michael said in agreement. JoAnn reluctantly excused herself and left the front counter for the back office while her husband, Michael, continued discussing with Boss and Lil Rick. She knew trouble was on the horizon when Lil Rick showed up because his specialty always involved someone losing their life. And just hearing Boss talk about snatching Jose's kids was enough to keep her awake at night. The plan was to find a way to kidnap Jose's oldest son, Levi, and hold him hostage until Mullins agreed to stop his search for Jose's daughter.

Michael knew this was a risky move but was already over his head. So he agreed to go along with the plan as long as no one was hurt. Boss gave Lil Rick a surveillance package with photos of Officer Mullins and his family. When Boss left the store, Michael was relieved that he was gone. He turned the open-for-business sign back on and yelled to the rear for JoAnn. When she returned to the storefront, she told Michael that he had to be careful when dealing with Boss and Lil Rick. "Yeah, I know," Michael replied as he and his wife hugged to comfort each other. But, unfortunately, the Brownings were again caught up in an illegal adoption scam that stemmed way back to the days of Mr. Kyle and Dr. Lewis. And now the biological mother has decided, after thirty years, that she wants to hold her child again.

Meanwhile, Officer Mullins and Dave decided to pay another visit to the place that would draw the most attention. And that place was Browning's Adoption Agency. When they walked in, Sarah Jenkins stood up at her desk. "It's you again, and I hope you know that you almost got me fired the last time you came in here poking your nose into God knows whatever. And don't think you're getting anywhere close to my files ever again," she added. "Just calm down, Miss Jenkins," Mullins replied. "I came by to apologize and to introduce my partner Dave. So come on over here, Dave," says Mullins. "Now didn't I tell you that she was the prettiest thing you ever did see," he said while pulling Dave closer to Sarah. "That you did say partner, and I have to agree," says Dave in a flirting manner. "Well, I guess you're not all that bad, Officer Mullins," says Sarah. But you're still not getting your hands on my files," she added. Officer Mullins looked at Sarah and smiled. "Well, I've done what I came to do, so I guess we'll be moving right along then," he responded. "Yeah, and you take care of your pretty self," Dave added. "You come back and see me sometimes. So you did say Officer Dave, right" She asked. "Just call me Dave for now," he said.

"What the hell was that, Dave," asked Mullins. "I was just playing along, partner," Dave said jokingly. "I hear you, partner. Just don't let me catch you trying to ease back over here to Miss Jenkins 'cause Deidre might not be so understanding," Mullins said jokingly. Meanwhile, as soon as they left the agency, Sarah was on the phone with Mrs. Browning. "Hello JoAnn, is Mr. Browning available," she asked. "Well, he's in the office. Can I help you" JoAnn asked. "I just want to let you all know that the GBI fellow came back to the agency, and I told him he wasn't touching anything," she explained. "You did good, Sarah, and I'll let Michael know," she said as she rushed to the office to inform Michael. "Officer Mullins paid another visit to the adoption agency," she said with a fearful voice. "Come over here, and don't you worry none," says Michael as he rested his chin on her head. He was confident that this would all be over when Mullins realized his actions were endangering his family.

Meanwhile, Mullins decided to call home and check on Jose and the kids. "How's my beautiful wife doing," he asked. "Your beautiful wife is fine, but she'd be much better if her husband would come home and take her to the supermarket," Jose replied. "Oh wow, I forgot all about it," said Mullins. "I'll be home in a couple of hours, and I'm all yours," he added. "I'm holding you to that, Mister, so don't be late," she said. After that, Mullins felt a lot better knowing that Jose was in a good mood. But little did they know that when she went out to check the mailbox, someone was stalking the house. Whoever it was, they were parked across the street and wearing black leather driving gloves. The stalker opened the glove box, pulled out a 9mm pistol, attached a silencer, and put it back into the glove box. Jose noticed the strange car parked in front of her home but didn't give it much thought.

Finally, after riding around Jackson, Georgia, and making their presence known, Mullins and Dave returned to the station to tighten loose ends and check their messages. After a while, Mullins decided to call it a day. "See you tomorrow, partner," he said. "Okay, man, later," Dave replied. On the way home, Mullins stopped by the flower shop and picked up some red roses for Jose. It was like a breath of fresh air, not followed by the white van anymore.

Jose was waiting for him with a passionate kiss when he entered the door. "Wow, do we have to go to the market today," he asked. "Yes, we do, so let's get the kids," she said. Mullins noticed a black Mercedes parked across the street when they backed out of the garage. He didn't want to upset Jose's mood, so he kept quiet. It had been a while, so he wanted to enjoy the moment. But when they pulled off, the stranger followed him to the supermarket. As Jose got out of the car, the stranger watched her closely. He seemed extremely angry by how he clutched his fist, tightly gripping the steering wheel with his black leather gloves. It was not the time for Officer Mullins to take his eyes off his wife or kids. The stranger was no doubt stalking Jose and her family. Shortly after Mullins and his family had entered the supermarket, Lil Rick showed up and entered the store. Boss had hired him to watch Jose's every move. But who was the stalker in the black Mercedes, and who hired him?

Finally, after shopping and loading the groceries, Mullins noticed the same black Mercedes parked across the parking lot. So he loaded up his family and left for home. Unfortunately, Lil Rick and the stranger in the black Mercedes were following him. This situation was growing into something dangerous, and Officer Mullins knew it. Somehow he had to find a way to convince Jose that she needed some help with the kids for a while. So when they got home, he unloaded the groceries and Lil Bobby. As the garage began to close, Mullins looked into the face of the stranger in the Mercedes. He was so bold that he pulled right up to the driveway. He even took the time to remove his shades as if he were saying, "Take a good look and remember my face." Mullins made a mental note of the black leather gloves and the dark shades because it was not cold enough for driving gloves. While he and Jose were putting the groceries away, he walked to the window to observe whether the guy was still there. And just as he suspected, he was still parked across the street, along with Lil Rick, who was parked about twenty yards away from the stranger. It appeared that Lil Rick had no idea who this strange person was either. When the stranger noticed Mullins watching from the window, he reached into his glove box and removed his 9mm pistol. Mullins decided to call Dave and inform him in case he needed backup. "Hey, partner," Mullins here. "Whenever you get a chance, I'd like you to drive by and check the plates of this black Mercedes parked outside my home. He followed me to the market," Mullins explained.

Dave agreed to check on the strange vehicle right away. When he arrived, he noticed that the Mercedes had Alabama tags. So he wrote down the tag number and called Mullins right away. "Hey dude, I'm outside your crib, and this guy has Alabama tags on his car." "Okay, thanks, partner," Mullins said. "You need me to check out old dude and see what's up before I leave," Dave asked. Nah, let's just see where it leads us, Mullins replied. Okay then," Dave said as he turned around and drove away. He wanted to go over and drag the guy out of his car and beat some answers out of him, but he promised Mullins that he would follow the rules. At least some of the rules.

While Dave was getting information on the Mercedes, Lil Rick was observing them both, trying to understand how they were connected. So he ran his background check on the strange vehicle. As it turned out, he was a professional hitman driving a stolen car with tag plates from Mobile, Alabama. So it was time to report the stranger to Boss. "Hey Boss, it seems we have an intruder who's also interested in the Mullins," said Lil Rick. "Find out who he is and get rid of him," said Boss. "And make sure you clean up behind yourself," he added. So now there was a change of plans. Lil Rick had to get rid of the stranger before he could finalize his kidnapping scheme. However, this might be easier said than done. They were both hired guns, and it would be a matter of who got who first.

The next morning when Mullins left for work, the stranger in the Mercedes followed, and Lil Rick followed the stranger. When Mullins arrived at the GBI station, the stranger turned off, and Lil Rick continued to follow him. He followed him to I-75 and on to a hotel in Locust Grove, Ga. This appeared to be his resting place, so Lil Rick waited until he went inside, then followed to see which room he entered. There was only one problem. The stranger had noticed Lil Rick following him before he entered the hotel. It was time to find out who Lil Rick was working for, so he entered his room and called his employer.

Shockingly, the stranger asked to speak to a senator. "Morning, mam. Is the senator available," he asked. "Yes, he is. Just one moment," his wife replied. When the senator answered the phone, the stranger told him of the problem with Lil Rick. "First of all, I told you never to call my home, and secondly, I need this problem to go away right now," he added. "Consider it done, sir," said the stranger. As it appeared, the Senator and Boss were on a collision course. Both had hired a hitman to stop the search for Jose's daughter. The Senator hired the stranger in the Mercedes to assassinate Mullins, and Boss hired Lil Rick to kidnap Levi. Boss wanted to keep his adopted daughter from her past. But the Senator from Alabama was married to Jose's daughter and did not want it publicized. And for a good reason. If his associates in the U.S. Congress had found out that his wife was illegally adopted and that she was a black woman, he could kiss his run for the Governor's office goodbye. Not to mention the social impact it would have on their two children. As for the two assassins, the collision was unavoidable due to a lack of communication between Senator Adams and Boss.

Meanwhile, Officer Mullins took to the streets for normal operations. And in general conversation, Dave offered to ask his fiancé if she would invite Jose out for a day of shopping and girl stuff. Mullins accepted it as a good idea and called Jose immediately. "Hey, pretty girl," Mullins says. "Okay, what have you done," Jose asked jokingly. "Nothing girl. Dave and I were talking, and he thought it might be a good idea if you and his fiancé did some girl stuff." "I'd like that very much," Jose replied. "Okay then, so be on the lookout for her call and remember her name is Deidre," says Mullins. "Got it," Jose responds. It seemed an excellent alternative since Jose was occupied with finding her daughter. Deidre called, and they had a great day of shopping.

They walked through the Mall and even had lunch in the food court. Deidre admired the life that Jose and Mullins had built. "I hope Dave and I can start a family one day," said Deidre. "Don't worry; your time will come?" Jose said. "And I thank you so much for taking time for the boys and me," she added. "So does that mean we can do it again," says Deidre jokingly. "It's a deal. Just call me and give me a heads up," Jose responded with a smile.

As for the stranger, it was 3 am and time to check on the competition. He needed to know if Lil Rick was still on surveillance in the parking lot. So he opened his gun case, pulled out a 9mm pistol with a silencer, and left the room through the side exit. When he got to the parking lot, he noticed that Lil Rick was asleep in his vehicle. This was too easy, he thought to himself but then again, why not. He pulled out the 9mm with the silencer and fired one shot to the head of Lil Rick. He observed momentarily to ensure that it was, in fact, a kill shot before returning to his room for a good night's sleep. The following day at 7 am, he checked out with no intention of returning. Lil Rick was found at shift change by hotel employees. He was found slumped over in his car with a gunshot wound to the head. Chief Wall of the Locust Grove Police Department was notified of the shooting, and the crime scene was roped off immediately. An APB was also initiated throughout the local counties within a 200 miles radius. The shooter was long gone and most likely looking for alternate transportation.

When Officer Mullins arrived at the GBI station the following day, he noticed an incident report with photos of the deceased car in the hotel parking lot. "Hey Dave, come over here," he said.

"What's up, partner" Dave replies. "This car is the same car that was following me around Butts County," says Mullins. "Damn, man, you're right," Dave said. The report stated that a man was dead in a Locust Grove hotel parking lot. "Are you thinking what I'm thinking?" says Mullins. "You know it, partner, let's ride," Dave replied. When they arrived at the Comfort Suite Hotel, they asked the front desk supervisor if they could review the parking lot surveillance tape. As they were being led to the video surveillance room to retrieve the tape, the Locust Grove police approached. "Just hold on a minute, cowboy," said Chief Wall. "This is still a local matter, and I don't recall inviting the state boys to the party," he added. "Well damn, John Wayne, we didn't mean to step on your toes," says Dave. "Come on, fellows," Mullins replies. "We're all here for the same reason, right?" While walking to the video room, Mullins whispers to Dave. "Leave these hillbillies alone before they kick our asses out." When they reviewed the tapes, it was evident that this was a professional hit. Mullins asked for an enhancement of the frame that showed the actual shooting. He looked at Dave; they knew it was the black Mercedes guy. The same guy who had followed Mullins to his driveway. "Okay, Chief, we'll leave the rest to you guys," said Mullins. "You just hold on a minute," said Chief Wall. "When does the GBI just walk away without being kicked off the crime scene?" "Why don't we start by telling me what Y'all know about the shooter," Chief Wall said. "Or I could lock both your asses up for 72 hours for withholding evidence," he added. "Okay, all we know is the shooter was seen around Butts County for the last day or so driving a black Mercedes with Alabama tags," Mullins replied. "So we're leaving now if it's okay with you guys," Dave said. "Yeah, right," Chief Wall replied. He knew that Officer Mullins and his partner had more information than they would share. For example, the fact that the Mercedes tags were reported stolen when Dave ran the license plates at Mullins's residence.

Meanwhile, the stranger had arrived at the Atlanta Airport, where he abandoned the black Mercedes and stole another vehicle. Eventually, it would be discovered and returned to the owner in Mobile, Alabama. Nevertheless, he had become invisible again because Mullins and Dave had no idea what he was driving. All they knew was that he had serious intentions. When Boss got word that Lil Rick had been shot execution-style, he started to worry that someone else was watching the situation. And he knew just where to look for answers. It was time he paid a visit to his wild and dangerous son-in-law, who had a reputation for making a mess of things. So he went to Alabama, where his daughter Amanda and the grandkids met him at the airport. "How's my little girl," says Boss as he hugs his daughter. They make small talk on the way to the house, but when they arrive, it is all about business for Boss and his son-in-law, Senator Adams. "What in the hell were you thinking, son? Why did you have Lil Rick hit? And don't say you didn't do it 'cause I know you," Boss said. "He got in the way, Boss, and I'm not about to lose everything I've built for some nigger. Especially my wife and kids," said the Senator. "Okay, that's over and done," said Boss. "But the plan was to kidnap one of the kids and use him as a bargaining chip against the Mullins. And since you've screwed it up, your guy will have to kidnap the kid," he said. "I've had about as much as I'm gone take from that damn Mullins fellow," Senator Adams said. "But I'll instruct my guy to grab the kid, and you better be ready to take him off my hands," he added. "I have a safe place to keep the kid until we work this whole mess out," Boss said. The search was getting more complicated by the hour, and now it seemed that Jose was further than ever from holding her daughter in her arms again. This thirty-year-old woman, who had been adopted in Jackson, Georgia, as a Jane Doe, had become the wife of a prominent White senator from Alabama.

Jane Doe had become Amanda Adams, and she would soon be the 1st Lady of the great state of Alabama. They had two beautiful kids and a lovely home. But would she even want to know her biological mother, or would she be so filled with a family tradition of hatred for people of color? If she had any of her mother's characteristics, this could be detrimental to her husband's campaign for the Governor's office. After all, she looked almost identical to her mother, Jose Mullins, and there would be no doubt in her or her children's minds once they saw their grandmother. Because just like her mother, Jose, Amanda's beauty was her trademark.

When Mullins got home from work, Jose told him how much she and the kids enjoyed spending the day with Deidre. "She's a nice person," said Jose. "Well, I'm glad you like her," Mullins replied. "Now tell me what's for dinner," he said. "Yeah, what's for dinner?" said Levi as he poked his head from behind the sofa. They looked at each other as if to say, "We got to be careful what we say with this little guy sneaking around." "Lucky he didn't catch his Dad being naughty," Jose replied. "I know that's right pretty lady," says Mullins as he leans over to kiss his beautiful wife. After dinner, he noticed Jose was taking extra time in the bathroom, so he poked his head in to see what she was doing. "Get out, nosey," she shouted. "Well, I just wanted to see what my wife was doing in the bathroom for so long. She might have another man in there, and I was going to ask if I could join them," he said jokingly. Then to his surprise, Jose came out and walked over to the bed. She was stunning. Even more beautiful than the first time he laid eyes on her. "You are so beautiful," Mullins said as he stood up, preparing to hold her. Jose walked closer to his bedside and slightly released the shoulder straps of the lovely red lace gown. His eyes followed the gown to the floor as if it had fallen in slow motion. He reached for her, but Jose wasn't having it. Tonight was her night, and she was determined to take complete control. She placed her finger over his lips as he started to speak. "I got this," said Jose as she pushed her husband back onto the bed. Her long silky hair stroked his chest as she climbed atop and made herself available for a night of pure passion.

The following day Mullins eased out of bed and prepared breakfast before going to work. When he was finished, he took his wife her breakfast tray and gave her a soft kiss. "Morning, honey," he said with a soft voice. "Why didn't you wake me," she asked. "Because you looked so peaceful," he replied as he sat the breakfast tray on the nightstand. And now I'm off for work," he added. "Call me later if you get a chance," she responded. When Mullins backed out of the garage, he hoped to see the stranger sitting out front.

This time he would bring the guy in for questioning because the video from the Comfort Suite hotel identified him as the shooter. The only leads Mullins had were the stranger and Lil Rick. And now, one was dead, and the other seemingly had vanished. He had no choice but to try and stir up the Browning family because it always seemed to bring out new leads. So back to the small town of Jackson, Georgia, it was. He decided to purchase from the gun store and hoped they would react to his purchase. When he walked into the store, he asked to see the Remington Pump Shotgun. When JoAnn Browning asked why he'd decided on purchasing a shotgun, he replied: "My wife is home alone, and I thought I might teach her to shoot." With that answer, JoAnn was speechless as she gave him a firearms form to fill out before the purchase was finalized. Mullins thanked JoAnn for assistance and left the store with his new shotgun and ammunition. It was almost impossible for him to keep a straight face while watching JoAnn turn White from fear. He wanted to laugh, but instead, he kept walking to his car. As soon as he pulled off, she called for Michael to come up front. "Wonder why he bought the gun," she asked. "There is no telling what that lunatic is up to, honey," Michael replied. "But I wish he'd shoot himself with it," he added as he gazed at Officer Mullins through the store window.

While driving back to the station, Mullins receives a call from Jose. She called to let him know that Deidre would pick her and the boys up again. "That's great, honey," he says. "You guys be careful out there and hold Levi's hand," Mullins insisted. When he arrived at the station, Dave followed up on some leads from the hotel shooting. Airport security had recovered the stolen black Mercedes that the shooter had previously used. And almost immediately, there was a report of another car stolen in that area. So Dave concluded that the shooter had abandoned one stolen car for another. And if so, it was only a matter of time before he would resurface at Mullin's residence. But when and if he did show his face, they would be waiting with handcuffs.

Meanwhile, Deidre has just arrived to pick up Jose and the boys for another shopping day. Only this time, the stranger was outside Jose's home, watching from across the street. For some unknown reason, he was always wearing those black driving gloves. When Deidre got out of her car, he took photos as she walked to the door. Jose opened the door. "Come on in; we're almost ready," she said. "Take your time cause we have all day," Deidre replied.

Finally, little Levi came out to make his presence known as usual "So you're gone take us on another trip today" he asked. "Yes, I am, if it's okay with you, Mister Levi," she replied jokingly. "Yeah, let's go, Mama," Levi yelled joyfully. "Here, let me get that bag, Jose," said Deidre as the couple left the house and loaded up in the car. When they pulled off, the stranger, who was now driving a black Ford SUV, followed them to the South Lake Mall. He walked behind them, hoping for a chance to grab little Levi. The ladies decided to stop at a Chinese food court for lunch, and Jose was very watchful because Mullins had told her to hold tight to Levi's hand. Levi was a friendly child by nature, which could be dangerous, especially with the stranger lurking around—waiting for an opportunity to snatch him away from his mother. Finally, after a couple of hours of window shopping, they decided it was time to leave. When they got to the car, Deidre began loading the bags in the trunk while Jose was putting Little Bobby in his car seat. Then all of a sudden, the stranger pulled up beside their car, got out, and snatched Levi. He quickly threw him inside the car and sped off. Jose and Deidre started screaming at the top of their lungs. But it was too late as the SUV left the parking lot. "Get in, Jose," said Deidre as she gave chase. "Call the police now, Jose," shouted Deidre. Jose was in shock and could not move, so Deidre called Dave. "Hey honey, some guy just kidnapped Levi," she said. "Oh, shit, partner, let's go," Dave shouted. "What's the description of the vehicle Deidre," he asked while running to the patrol car. "I'm driving," said Mullins. "Where are they" he added. "South Lake Mall area, and he's driving a black Ford SUV," Deidre replied. "Thanks, honey. " Dave responded, take care of Jose and Bobby, and tell her we're all over it," Dave responded. "Okay, this would be a good time to tell me why you asked Deidre to take care of my wife and child. Talk to me, Dave," Mullins said with a frightened look. "They got Levi, partner," Dave replies as he violently checks his 9mm ammo clip. "Okay, game on," Mullins responded. Dave quickly called in an "APB" alert to all surrounding areas. This was the worst thing that could ever have happened. Deidre drove as fast as she could until, finally, she almost hit a pickup truck head-on. "Pull over, Deidre, he's gone," said Jose. "I said pull over, Deidre," Jose shouted as she gave attention to little Bobby in the rear car seat. Deidre suddenly realized how dangerous it was to continue chasing the kidnapper. So she pulled over and called Dave. She was shaking like a leaf as she tried to explain to Dave what had happened. "Calm down, honey," he said. "We have cops in the air and on the ground. And we're going to find this guy," he promised. "Mullins and I are in your area right now, so what else can you tell me about the occupants," Dave asked. "All I know is that we saw one White guy wearing black gloves pull up in a new model Ford SUV and snatch Levi," she explained. Dave instructed Deidre to drive to the station, where a Task Force would escort them home. Officers would also remain posted outside the residence until relieved by Officer Mullins.

Meanwhile, Mullins is equally concerned about Jose's mental state, so he hurries to the station to try and comfort her. Captain Mack met them at the door when they got to the station. "In my office, guys," he says. When they sat down, the Captain explained that this kidnapping case needed to be handled by someone who was not involved. That's when Officer Mullins told the Captain, "You can stop right there because there is no way in hell I will stop looking for my damn son," Mullins shouted. "And if you don't start talking and tell me everything you know, I'm going to Internal Affairs," he added. "Come clean, Captain," Dave said. After sitting quietly for a while, the Captain decided to come clean with the guys he'd come to know and trust over the years. "Okay, guys, here's the deal. It stems from your wife giving birth to a baby girl and how the child was adopted some years ago," says Captain Mack.

"August 1946, to be exact," Mullins said in an interruptive manner. "Yes, 1946. Captain Mack confirmed. "Anyway, she was adopted without Jose's consent by a very prominent family who does not want the child to know her biological parents. "Biological parent, my ass," says Mullins. "I'll tell you what they don't want. They don't want the good White folk to know that their precious little daughter has a black mother. A fifteen-year-old black mother who begged in tears for many years. Begging day and night for that nasty bastard of a father, Kyle, to bring back the baby girl he ripped from her arms. A black mother who loves her daughter very much. So much that, thirty years later, she still cries herself to sleep on my shoulder. On my damn shoulder, Captain," says Mullins with tears in his eyes. "She wants to hold her child, Captain," he added with a passionate plea.

Captain Mack and Dave both listened with tears welling in their eyes. Mullin's passionate plea sparked the beginning of a task where failure was not an option. "Okay, guys, we need a transfer warrant to bring those lousy low lifers to justice," says Captain Mack. "You get the warrants, and we'll get them served, sir," says Dave. "So what are we saying, guys," Mullins said. "Looks like we're on our way to Alabama, dude," Dave answers with a smile. Mullins thanked the Captain for his honesty and hurried home to try and comfort Jose.

Chapter 6: Jose's Memory Loss

After a long day, Officer Mullins has to go home and face a traumatized wife. When he arrives, he finds Jose sitting on the sofa and staring at the wall. He sat beside her and called her name, but she didn't respond. "How long has she been this way," he asked. "She hasn't spoken a word since we got here," Deidre replied. "I'll be taking her to the Learning Center to have her evaluated by her doctor, and I was hoping that you could attend to little Bobby for a few days," Mullins said. "I'd be happy to help in any way I can," Deidre replied. "Dave and I will be leaving for Mobile, Alabama, tomorrow, and I was hoping that you would take Bobby home with you until I return," Mullins said as he broke down in tears. Deidre does her best to console Mullins but simultaneously feels helpless as she watches her friend, Jose, sit in pure silence, unaware of her surroundings. "You should take Jose now," Deidre says to Mullins. He turns to his wife and takes her by the hand, leading her to the car. Dave and Deidre gather some of Little Bobby's things and leave for home. "Sometimes I wonder just how much Mullins can take before he breaks," Dave says to Deidre as they head home.

As for Jose, she didn't say a word while driving to the Learning Center, and when they arrived, Dr. Price was waiting in her office. Mullins was confused when he asked Jose if she was okay. "Honey, are you okay," Mullins asked. "Of course I am, and why wouldn't I be" Jose responded with a smile. Mullins handed Dr. Price a copy of the kidnapping report along with the order of events. When she read that their son had been kidnapped earlier that day, she suspected that Jose was suffering a mental relapse. She looks at Mullins and extends her hand. "I will call you when I know more," says Dr. Price. Mullins looks at his wife, holds her hands, and tells her he will be back. He tried desperately to hold back the tears. He could see that Jose did not know about ever leaving the Learning Center; even worse, she did not know about ever starting a family. It meant that she had no memory of giving birth to Levi or Bobby. And it gets worse as he realizes she had no present knowledge of their wedding day when she yells out, "Don't forget our wedding is only days away." Mullins turned and headed to his car, and with tears running down his face, he made a vow to Jose and the boys to leave no stone unturned. He needed to find Levi and arrest the kidnapper and everyone involved. He called Dave to ensure the warrants were ready and the flight plans were in order. The time was now, and the gloves were off. Boss and his wicked crew had awakened Officer Mullin's, inner man. It was game on.

Dave was proud of Deidre for assuming responsibility for Little Bobby. "So you gone do the Mama thing for a few days, huh, he said jokingly." "And I'm assuming you understand that we're going to Alabama tomorrow," he added. "Yes, I do, and I'm gone need more than a handshake before you go, mister man, " she replied with a sexy attitude. "So give me a few minutes to put the baby down, and I'll be right with you." Dave pretended to be excited, but his mind was already in Mobile, Alabama. The clock was ticking for Mullin's son with no time to waste. He knew that the first forty-eight hours were critical for any chance of recovery.

The following day Mullins was there on time and ready to go. "Hey, partner, you want to stop by Deidre's and see little Bobby before we go," Dave asked. "It is bad luck to say goodbye to the ones you love," Mullins responded. Okay, let's do this," says Dave. When they arrived at the Atlanta airport, they checked the baggage and boarded the flight. And now they were off to Mobile, Alabama, with very high hopes of finding Levi and bringing him back home safe and unharmed. Even though they were following a lead on the shooter at the Comfort Suite Hotel, the mission was to get everybody involved back to Georgia to stand trial. It was more likely than not that the kidnapper had taken Levi to Alabama, where he would be held captive by Boss's crew until Mullins decided to stop his search for Jose's daughter. But at this point, that was wishful thinking because Officer Mullins had no choice but to find Levi and Jose's illegally adopted daughter. And time was never more critical. They finally landed in the great state of Alabama. After gathering their luggage and a rental car, they went to the hotel and checked in. While Mullins was checking in, Dave asked the desk clerk if she knew a man named Jack

Wallace (aka Boss). "Everybody around here knows Mr. Wallace," she said. "He owns a nightclub here, and that would be the best place to catch up with him," she added. "Does this club have a name?" Mullins asked. "The Flamingo," she said. "That figures, Mullins replied. "Yep, a sleazy business for a sleazy man," Dave hinted. After settling in their adjoined rooms, they had dinner at the hotel and headed to the Flamingo Lounge. As it seemed the hotel clerk omitted to tell the GBI duo that Jack Wallace, aka Boss, also owned the hotel. And it was as if the desk clerk had instructions because she called the Flamingo lounge and told the club manager that two police officers from Georgia had checked in and coming their way. The hotel employees would make Mullin's job even more difficult because now somebody is informed each time they leave the hotel. When they arrived at the Flamingo Lounge, Mullins asked the bartender if Jack Wallace was there. The bartender replied by asking Officer Mullins if he had an appointment. Of course, Mullins responded by showing his badge. "This is my appointment. Now, where is he?" The bartender waved for club security to come over to the bar. "Show this nice policeman upstairs to Mr. Wallace," he said. As Officer Mullins turned to inform his partner that he was going upstairs, he noticed that Dave had a ringside seat and a fist full of dollar bills as he was enjoying an evening of dirty dancing. But his fun is short-lived as Mullins goes over and taps him on the shoulder, reminding his fearless partner that they have work to do. "Come on, man, I was just getting warmed up," says Dave. "I'll be back, ladies," Dave shouts as he waves his fist full of dollar bills at the topless dancers. Mullins looks at Dave and shakes his head. "You are one crazy White boy," he says as they follow security upstairs to meet the man called Boss. "Come on in, gentlemen," says Boss. "It's not every day I get a visit from the police." "Well, I do hope the love affair continues after I serve you with this transfer warrant," Mullins said as he handed Jack Wallace the warrant. "Who in the hell do you think you are to come into my place of business and serve me with this worthless piece of paper? Get my damn lawyer in here," Boss says to club security.

When his attorney entered the room, he examined the transfer warrant and found it in order. It was a warrant to appear before a grand jury for questioning. "I'm sorry, Mr. Wallace, but the judge has signed this warrant, and these two GBI agents had the authority to bring you back to the state of Georgia. So there, you will appear before the judge, and he will hear your case. "In other words, Mr. Jack Wallace, you're coming back to the great state of Georgia with us," says Officer Mullins. "And don't even think about calling in any favors from your politician friends," Dave added.

When Mullins and Dave left with Boss in custody, Attorney Gibbs called Senator Sam Adams. "Good evening Senator," says Attorney Gibbs. "They got Boss," he added. "Dammit. I've had about as much as I'm gone take from that Mullins fellow," he said. "Well, if you don't stop him before he departs the state of Alabama, you may not be able to stop him," said Attorney Gibbs. "I'll see what I can do about getting the warrant reversed," the Senator replied. He called the Judge there in Mobile and asked if he could place a hold on the transfer, but it was too late. Officer

Mullins and Dave were already headed to the airport with their prize catch. Jack Wallace, aka Boss, was on his way to Georgia to face illegal adoption and murder charges, if possible. Boss knew that someone in his circle had talked to the authorities. He had a reputation for dealing with traitors that were second to none in the world of crime.

When the flight arrived at the Atlanta airport, Captain Mack was waiting at the terminal with a state vehicle. Boss didn't know what to make of the Captain's presence. He was under the impression that he was still a team player. But now it seemed that Captain Mack was the traitor. And this time, justice prevailed as the Captain read him his rights and told him that he was charged with illegal adoption practices. "You nigger loving bastards think you can hold me," Boss shouted? "If you haven't noticed, you are in Georgia and on your way to jail," said Mullins. But little did they know, help was on the way as usual. And by the time Boss finished processing for lockup, Attorney Gibbs was there with a bond signed by the state court judge. "How in the hell did you get here so fast," asked Officer Mullins. "Private jets are made to keep me one step ahead of your country, hicks," Gibbs responded? "And now I'll be taking Mr. Jack Wallace off your hands," he added as he winked at Mullins.

"Like hell, you will," Dave replied in anger. "Take the cuffs off, guys. Mr. Wallace has been released by the state courts and is free to go," said Captain Mack. As Boss left the station, he whispered to Captain Mack, "Always place your bets on the Boss, son." Captain Mack was speechless as he turned and walked away.

He knew that somehow Boss would escape the charges if they didn't find new leads. He was also aware that his future with the Bureau would be short-lived if he didn't finish Boss off for good. And Officer Mullins and Dave would suffer the same fate if they failed to obtain new evidence against Boss's Empire. The good Senator from Alabama had called in a favor to GBI Headquarters, and things were going sour for the dynamic GBI duo.

Meanwhile, Mullins had a lot on his plate. His wife was still at the Learning Center, and his newborn was still with Deidre. "Okay, Dave, I appreciate all your help, man and if you do me a favor, tell your girl Deidre that I'll pick little Bobby up as soon as I return from checking on the wife," Mullins said. "Not a problem, partner. Just take whatever time you need," Dave replied. When Mullins arrived, to his surprise, he found that Jose was doing fine and ready to come home. She ran over to hug him as soon as he entered her room. "Don't ever leave me here again?" Jose said. Mullins thanked Dr. Price for everything she'd done and asked if there were any special instructions. "Well, there is one thing that I would like to recommend," said Dr. Price. "Take it easy on the drama," she said jokingly. Mullins was so happy to be taking his wife home in her right mind. "So how's it coming with finding Levi, and where is Bobby" Jose asked. She was in high gear when they walked out of the Learning Center. She was ready to pick up Bobby and start her search for Levi. "Just leave it to me to search for Levi," Mullins said. "Listen to me," said Jose. "They took my son, and you say leave it to me? I will not rest until I have him back. So don't even think about shutting me out," she added. "I am only trying to protect you and Bobby," Mullins explained as he headed to Deidre's house to pick up little Bobby. When they arrived, Jose walked in and gave Deidre a big hug. "Thank you so much for keeping little Bobby," Jose said. "You are so welcome," Deidre replied. She had gotten used to holding little Bobby over the last couple of days and now wanted one of her own. From how she looked at Mullins, it appeared that what she wanted was what Jose had. And it showed as she gave Mullins an extended friendly hug. When they got in the car, Jose told Mullins jokingly, "Easy on the hugs, big fellow."

"Come on now. Are you kidding? "Well, she did hold the hug a little longer than normal," said Jose. "I'm gone; just pretend I didn't hear that," Mullins replied as they headed home. Would this be the beginning of marital problems for Jose? She was no expert in infidelity, but it didn't take a rocket scientist to figure out that her new friend was making a move for her husband. Only time will tell. When they got home, it was sadness in every room of the house. "How can we be whole without him," said Jose. "I promise you with every ounce of my being that I will not rest until our son is home," Mullins replied. Jose had never seen him so helpless. "God will deliver," Jose said as she wiped the tears from his face. To hide his pain, Mullins kneeled to play with Bobby. "Tonight, little man, you're sleeping with me," he said. "As long as he's not in the middle," Jose added jokingly. Overall, it was a sad day for the Mullins, but they still had each other.

Meanwhile, Boss is on his way back to Alabama on his private jet, where he will relax and forget about the charges in Georgia. But to his surprise, Captain Mack had assigned an undercover agent to follow him to Alabama and report his every move. When Boss arrived at the airport in Alabama, he stepped off the plane with a big smile. He looked at Attorney Gibbs and said: "Next time that nigger Mullins comes to Alabama, he won't leave." And the same goes for his nigger loving partner. As it seemed, the Boss was untouchable and above the law, especially in Mobile, Alabama, where political favors were bought. But the following day, when he left home for the office, the undercover cop followed him like a shadow, hoping that he would lead him to little Levi. The day was going slow until around three o'clock in the afternoon when a black Limo pulled up and parked at the front entrance of the Flamingo Bar. A few minutes later, club security came out to meet the driver of the Limo. The undercover cop immediately called Captain Mack. "I think we got something, sir," he said as he observed. "There's some strange activity between club security and a Limo driver," he added. "Just keep your eyes on that Limo and keep this line open," Captain Mack said. "Hold on, Captain, you are not going to believe this, but a black kid that fits the description of Officer Mullins son just got out of the Limo, and he's being led into the club by security," he said. "Okay, let him take the kid inside before arresting the Limo driver. Search him for weapons and phones. We can't allow him to alert the guys inside the bar. The Mobile Swat Team is on the way," said Captain Mack. They're coming in soft, so stay alert," he added.

As soon as security entered the club with the kid, the undercover agent approached the Limo driver. He read him his rights while walking him to his patrol car and cuffed him. When the SWAT team arrived, the undercover agent gave them the details and custody of the Limo driver. "We'll take it from here," said the SWAT Captain. With the Flamingo club surrounded, the SWAT team entered and began searching for three-year-old Levi. As expected, Boss was alerted as soon as Swat made their entry. He followed their movement using the security camera in his office. He knew they would come directly to his office, so he told security to take the kid out of the rear entrance. But the undercover agent waited when club security walked out the back entrance. "Police, don't you move," he said. The security guy raised his hands and stood still. "Come on over here to me, kid. What's your name, little fellow" he asked. My name is Levi, and I want my Mama," he said.

The situation seemed to be under control until the club security guy suddenly reached for his pistol. That's when the undercover agent pushed the kid away and fired three shots. The security guy was killed with his gun in his hand. The secret agent immediately placed Levi in the patrol car and called 911 for an ambulance. He also called for the local police force to rope off the area while he secured little Levi. It was time to call Captain Mack with the good news. "Hey, Captain, the kid is in my custody," he said. "Good job, bring him home," said Captain Mack with a smile. He called Officer Mullins immediately with the good news. When Mullins heard that Levi was safe, he started crying. "What's wrong?" Jose said as she took the phone from Mullin's hand. "Hello, who is this," she asked.

"It's Captain Mack, and we've found your son," he said. Jose didn't know what to say. She quickly grabbed little Bobby's car seat and ran to the car. Mullins was right behind her. When they arrived at the station, Captain Mack was waiting. "We got him," he said. Mullins and Jose were excited but very nervous because Levi was still in Mobile, Alabama. "Okay, Captain, spit it out. Who took my son" asked Mullins. "We're not certain yet, but he was found at the Flamingo," he answered. "Let me bring him in, sir," Mullins requested. "You know better than that. You're too close to the case, and we're not blowing this one," Captain Mack replied. "But undercover is bringing Levi home as we speak," he added.

Meanwhile, the SWAT Team arrested Jack Wallace (aka Boss) for his involvement in the kidnapping. But, of course, he denied knowing anything about it. And the only person who could witness his participation was the club security guy, who had been shot and killed at the rear entrance by the undercover agent. However, one other person could connect Boss to the kidnapping. And that was the Limo driver who brought little Levi to the Flamingo club. He was already in police custody, but he wasn't talking. Instead, he asked for an attorney as he was arrested and released immediately on bail. When Senator Adams heard about the raid at the Flamingo, he knew immediately that Officer Mullin's son was in police custody. So he started to cover his tracks by calling Attorney Gibbs. "Okay, so they got Boss. There's nothing we can do now but get rid of the hired shooter. I want him out of the country if possible," he said. "Consider it done," Attorney Gibbs replied. While Attorney Gibbs was busy making arrangements to get the kidnapper out of the country, the undercover cop was boarding a flight to Georgia with little Levi.

When they arrived at the airport, Officer Mullins and Jose, along with Captain Mack, Dave, and Deidre, were also waiting. Seeing Levi reunited with his Mom and Dad was the most beautiful sight. The entire welcoming committee had wet eyes. The Captain smiled, turned his attention to the undercover agent, and introduced him to the Mullins and Jose. His name was Officer Sanchez from the division north of Atlanta. Captain Mack was more determined than ever to bring Boss and his corrupt crew down. Of course, this would be a tall task considering the state of Alabama was still very much in control of everyone arrested during the raid at the Flamingo Bar. It would take some time for a grand jury to determine what charges would be filed against Boss. The fact that he didn't physically possess the kidnap victim would weigh heavily in his favor.

Meanwhile, the Mullins were joined by Dave and Deidre, who followed them to the parking deck. When they got to their cars, Deidre hugged Jose. "Thanks again," said Jose as they loaded up and headed home. Dave knew the work had just begun, and these guys were not playing around. He knew that now was not the time for a victory lap, but he also knew that his partner needed some space. However, they both knew it was never good practice to slow down or back off an investigation when there was a significant break in the case. And most likely, finding Jose's long-lost daughter was at their fingertips. The only problem was who and what they would encounter when they got back to Mobile. It would not be easy for the two GBI detectives who vowed to bring the bad guys to justice.

While driving home, Dave asked Deidre if she was hungry, but she didn't answer. She was still thinking about her time with little Bobby and how lucky Jose was to have a family. "Are you with me, or am I riding with a ghost?" Dave asked jokingly. "I'm sorry. What did you say" Deidre asked. Dave could see that something was heavy on her mind, but he had no idea what it was. Deidre had thoughts of envy for the life that Mullins and Jose had built over the short time together. She and Dave had been together even longer and never a whisper about marriage or kids. She wanted what Jose had, and the thoughts were cemented in her mind.

"So what are we having for dinner," Dave asked. "I thought we might get carried out on the way home if that's okay," she responded. "Sounds good to me," Dave said with a confused look. He was beginning to see a change in Deidre, which could cause a problem for the two guys who had been partners for years. Could Deidre control her desires and admiration for her new friend's husband and family? When Dave stopped to pick up carryout, Deidre suggested they get enough for the Mullins. Dave paused for a moment. "Well, I guess you could call Jose," he said. Dave could tell that Deidre was eager to visit Mullins and Jose, but he didn't know why. Deidre called Jose while Dave went inside to order the carryout. "Hello, Jose, Dave and I are getting carry-out, and we thought you might want to share." Jose hesitated before answering. "Thanks, Deidre, but we're just putting the kids down. It's been an exhausting day," says Jose.

"But a rain check would be nice," she added. "Oh my God, where are my manners" Deidre responded. "You are so right, and we will call you guys later," she added. She quickly went inside to let Dave know they would order two. Meanwhile, Jose looks at Mullins with a confused look on her face. "What's wrong," he asked. "Deidre just called to ask if we wanted to share carry out," Jose said. "Whatever you say is fine with me," Mullins replied. "Tonight," Jose asks as she crosses her arms. "What are you talking about, girl? You better get over here so I can enjoy private time with my wife," Mullins said jokingly. When Jose continued to stand with her arms folded, Mullins finally saw that she was serious. He walked over to Jose and put his arms around her, and assured her that she was the only woman for him. But now he begins to wonder if there was any substance to what Jose was thinking about Deidre or if it was just a woman thing. So he said to Jose, "If it continues, I'll speak to Dave. Now, may I please have some private time with my wife" he added.

Two days later, when Mullins returned to work, Dave was waiting with a plan forward in the search for Jose's daughter. "Okay, partner, what you got," Mullins asked." "Well, I thought we might start with a list of Jack Wallace's relatives. He seems to be everywhere the case leads us," Dave said. "Yeah, I know, but what could be his interest," Mullins asked. They decided to pay another visit to the adoption agency, and hopefully, Ms. Sarah Jenkins would be in a talkative mood. When they walked into the agency,

Sarah immediately called her employer, Michael Browning, to inform him that the GBI was at the agency. "Do you call in for all of your visitors?" Dave asked jokingly. "Not usually," said Sarah. "Only when I got people who meddle in other people's business," she added. While Sarah and Dave made small talk, Mullins kept watch on the parking lot, and sure enough, Michael Browning pulled into the parking lot. He appeared angry that Officer Mullins and Dave were still snooping around his adoption agency. "Don't you people have something better to do than put your nose in my business?" he asked angrily. "We do not," Dave replied. "Listen, Mr. Browning, all we want is some information on the adoption of my wife's daughter, and we will be out of your business for good," says Officer Mullins. Michael Browning responded by asking them to leave his place of business and requested that they contact his attorney with any further questions. "And who would that be, Mr. Browning" Mullins asked. "His name is Attorney Gibbs," Michael replied. "Have a nice day, Mr. Browning?" Mullins said. After learning that Boss and Browning shared the exact attorney, they were almost sure that the Browning Adoption Agency was the starting point for finding Jose's long-lost daughter. And Attorney Gibbs was a link that would soon connect the dots.

When they returned to the station, Captain called them into his office. "We got trouble, guys," he said. "What kind of trouble," Dave asked. "The Limo driver made bail," Captain Mack said. "And it gets worse," he added. "How much worse," Mullins asked. "It appears that after his release, someone decided to put a bullet in his head execution style." "Dammit," says Dave. "So they spring him from jail, then execute him before he talks," says Mullins. "And let me guess. The only people who can tie Jack Wallace (aka Boss) to the kidnapping of my son are dead. First, the security guard and now the Limo driver. And that murdering pig might be set free. No way, Captain," shouts Mullins. "You listen to me, Mullins. I will handle this case my way, and I don't need a loose cannon out there blowing things up," he replied. "Now, both of you get your minds right because Mobile, Alabama, will not be a cakewalk from this point on.

Captain Mack was almost sure that with both witnesses deceased, chances for an indictment of Jack Wallace were slim. Especially in the state of Alabama, where his son-in-law was a powerful U.S. Senator and the people's choice for the Governor's Mansion. It was only a matter of time before the kidnapping of Mullin's son would be blamed on the two men who were already deceased. Attorney Gibbs gave one last assignment to the shooter before sending him back to Australia. And that assignment was to eliminate Michael and JoAnn Browning immediately. They were the only ones who knew of Levi's kidnapping that resulted in Lil Rick's death. It would be clear sailing for Boss and his son-in-law after the Brownings were eliminated. His worst nightmare was for Jose Mullins to make contact with his daughter. Even worse, if she ever learned that her biological mother was black. Jack Wallace would stop at nothing to prevent that from happening, and the Brownings in Jackson, Georgia, were about to find out just how serious he was about keeping his secret.

JoAnn Browning opened the store doors the following day and noticed a strange man sitting out front. She knew most of the customers but didn't recognize this person. He got out of his car and went inside to browse around. After a few minutes, she asked if he needed assistance. He told her that he was only browsing and left the store. After a while, her husband, Michael, came in and began unloading cases of merchandise from his truck. JoAnn walked over to tell him about the stranger. "Not now, honey, I'm busy, he said. "But Michael, I got a creepy feeling about this strange guy this morning," she replied. "What strange guy," he asked, with a scary look on his face. JoAnn began telling her husband about the stranger, and he quickly turned the Open sign off and locked the door. "We're closed for the day. Let's go," he said. JoAnn was frightened by his demeanor and hurried to the back office for her purse. They left the store and headed for home. JoAnn was even more frightened because of the urgency to close the shop. "I'm scared, Michael," she said with teary eyes. Michael remained silent while focusing on a strange sports car in his rearview mirror. Finally, he asked his wife what kind of car the stranger was driving. When she told him it was a black 1975 Corvette, he knew right away that it was Boss's hitman doing cleanup work, and he wasn't going down without a fight. "Don't turn around; we're being followed," he said. The hired shooter from Australia had dumped the stolen Ford SUV used for the kidnapping of Levi and was now driving a stolen black 1975 Corvette. He was as skilled at stealing cars as he was at killing people execution style.

When Michael arrived at his residence, he turned into his driveway and told JoAnn to get down into the truck's floor. The stranger pulled in behind them and casually got out of his car. He was secretly carrying a 9mm under his jacket. Michael was watching in his rearview mirror as he tucked it away. He waited until the hired hitman was even with the truck's rear end before opening the door and firing several shots, killing the stranger. Two years earlier, Michael was by a gun dealer. He took the threat seriously and decided to rig the truck door with an automatic rifle for a time such as this. It was installed in the driver's door with the trigger exposed near the door handle, rigged so that anyone approaching from the rear would be in the line of fire when he opened the door. And it finally paid off because the shooter had met his match, and Attorney Gibbs would not need the airline's ticket to Australia. As for Boss, he had made a big mistake in going after Michael and JoAnn Browning because they knew the whole story of the illegal adoption of Jose's child in August of 1946. And now it was almost sure they would become witnesses for the state. Boss had made an enemy that he would soon regret.

Michael quickly picked his frightened wife up and carried her into the house. He told her to stay put while he went outside to assess the situation. As he approached the shooter, he noticed a 9mm pistol in his waist. It was tucked under his jacket. Michael knew immediately that he and his wife had escaped death by a narrow margin. He also knew the intended hit had Boss's name all over it. So instead of calling Sheriff Wallace, Boss's cousin, he called one of the deputies. It allowed the deputy time to secure the crime scene before Sheriff Wallace could rid the area of evidence that might lead back to his cousin Jack Wallace. Things were heating up, and suddenly, the quiet southern town of Jackson, Georgia, had once again become the center of attention and battleground for the criminally insane. The Brownings could only sit and watch as the ambulance collected the remains of the deceased stranger while their confused neighbors gathered around. When Sarah got news of the shooting, she started locking all the file cabinets and shutting down all computers at the Adoption Agency. She knew it would only be a matter of time before the police arrived. She planned to close up shop, go home and let the Brownings take care of their mess. She'd had enough of the GBI detectives, Mullins and Dave, snooping around and asking questions. There was already talk around town that the state police were investigating the Browning Adoption Agency, and the shooting at the Browning residence would invite their return.

Meanwhile, Mullins and Dave were preparing to return to Mobile, Alabama, when they received a call concerning the shooting. They were sure it was the same shooter from the hotel parking lot in Locust Grove. When they finally arrived, the deceased was already in the ambulance and prepared for transport to the county morgue. "Hold up," Mullins shouted to the ambulance driver. "Okay, cowboy, this is my rodeo," said Sheriff Wallace. "It may be your rodeo," says Officer Mullins, "But I'm checking this cargo," he added. "Why the hell not? Go ahead and interview the poor bastard. He can't tell you much," Sheriff Wallace said as he walked away, chuckling as if it were funny. "Ok, deputies gather around over here. Dick Tracey and his Buddy gone be taking over this mess. So let's pack it up and let them have it," the Sheriff added. Officer Mullins paid no attention to the sarcasm and continued to search for clues that might lead to the person that hired the assassin. "Hey partner, over here" yelled Dave as he pointed to a file in the victim's car. It was a file on Michael and JoAnn Browning. "The state is confiscating, Okay Sheriff, this vehicle and the contents as evidence in an ongoing investigation," says Officer Mullins.

"Like hell it is. It would help if you boys left," the Sheriff said as he realized they'd found evidence. The Sheriff was briefly interrupted by a phone call. When he noticed the call was from his cousin Boss, he walked away from Mullins and Dave. "I'm gone take this call, and don't nobody touch a damn thang til I get back," he added. He walked over and got into his patrol car to return the call. Officer Mullins and Dave had an Idea that the call was from someone wanting to know the status of the shooting. "What in the hell have you done? I got a dead body here, and the damn GBI is all over it. You better stay your ass clear, Boss," he said. "Oh hell, don't you worry none. That's just one less witness I gotta worry about. Where is the hell, Michael and JoAnn? Boss asked. "You listen to me. The Brownings are your least worry right now. I gotta go clean up your damn mess," the Sheriff said as he angrily hung up the phone.

He walked back over to the victim's car and opened the door. "Hold up here, Sheriff," Dave said as he leaned against the door to prevent entry. "We got orders to wait for the Captain." "This is my county, and I'm in charge here," the Sheriff responded. "As I said, cowboy. Hands off until my Captain arrives, Dave repeated. Finally, Captain Mack and his forensic team arrived and began taking prints and photos. The collected data was ready for downloading in the Mobile Laboratory.

Within minutes it was determined that the photo of the deceased matched the photo of the shooter at the Locust Grove shooting. "It's all your Sheriff," Dave said as he walked away. Sheriff Wallace was confident that the laboratory reports would lead the GBI investigators straight to Jack Wallace and eventually to Senator Adams in Mobile, Alabama. Mullins and Dave walked over to the Brownings and asked them if they would make a statement. "Don't tell me you're still willing to protect that double-crossing Jack Wallace?" Dave asked. JoAnn started to speak, but Michael quickly told her to hush up. "Okay, Michael has it your way, but he may not miss next time," Mullins warned. According to the look on JoAnn's face, it was obvious that they were both frightened and very nervous. There was no doubt that they would turn states evidence. The only question was who they would trust with their statements. Michael knew that Boss had a mole in every police station from Georgia to Alabama, and every politician seemed to be for sale. When Officer Mullins left, he turned to his wife and said, "Boss ain't the only one with a gun, little darling. And if it comes down to him or us, I will blow his fat ass away." Michael Browning was in survival mode.

Officers Mullins and Dave returned to the station but decided to visit Sarah Jenkins at the adoption agency. When they arrived, she was locking up. They watched as she walked to her car. She was so nervous she could hardly open the car door. "Are you okay, Ms. Sarah?" Dave asked. She just stood there, unable to move. Her body trembled with fear. Dave got out of the car and walked over to see if she was ok. As he approached, he noticed she'd been crying. He put his arms around her to comfort her and realized she was shaking. He took the keys from her hand and told Mullins to follow him. "Get in, Sarah. I'm driving you home because you are in no shape to drive," Dave told her. While driving home, she was silent until she asked: "Are they going kill me too?" "Nobody's gone kill anybody, Sarah," Dave responded. He also told her that it would be a good idea to stay away from the adoption agency for a couple of days. At least until the air cleared; when they arrived at her house, Dave got out and walked her to her door. He assured her that the shooting was an isolated incident and had nothing to do with her.

During the drive back to the station Mullins asked Dave if he thought the deceased guy was the kidnapper. "I don't think it matters," says Dave. "Yeah, you're right, and I won't rest until I find the person who hired him," Mullins replied. They were close to solving the case, but there was no doubt that Boss and Attorney Gibbs would blame everything on the deceased. The Captain was already planning the next move when they walked into the station. "Come on in here guys. We still got work to do," he said. Tomorrow we will launch a full investigation of the entire Jack Wallace team, including his cousin Sheriff Wallace. So go home and rest because you are returning to Mobile, Alabama."

Captain Mack had seen enough corruption from Boss and his crew and was about to unleash everything in his arsenal, even if it meant early retirement. It was almost sickening to watch as Sheriff Wallace did all he could to cover up the criminal actions of his cousin Boss. He'd spent his life fighting for what was right, and now he was challenged by the same system he'd raised his right hand to uphold and defend. Officer Mullins and Dave were not just his subordinates but also his friends. And now he was sending them into a hostile environment where they would have only a slim chance of coming back alive because Boss and his son-in-law wanted the both of them eliminated.

When Mullins got home, to his surprise, Dave's girlfriend, Deidre, was parked outside. When he walked in the door, Levi ran over for a hug. Mullins picked his son up and reached for his wife. He hugged them both and gave them the good news about the kidnapper. "Well, ladies, you can rest your tired minds now," said Mullins. The bad guy is dead," he added. Jose's face lit up like a Christmas tree. Deidre came over to share in the celebration of the good news. The closer she got to Mullins, the harder it was to hide her feelings. Everything he did, from showing affection for his family to the smell of his cologne, seemed to turn her on even more. Finally, Jose saw her hand resting a little low on Mullin's lower back. And Deidre was in no hurry to move it. "Let me walk you out, Deidre," Jose said politely. When the two ladies got outside, Jose turned to Deidre and thanked her again for being there for her and the kids. "You are welcome, girlfriend," Deidre replied. Then as the car drove off into the dark, Jose watched as she shook her head as if to say, "I can't believe she did that right in front of me."

She returned to the house and gave her husband a short kiss on the chin. "If I see that woman squeezing your butt one more time, I'm going break her hand," she said with a smile. Mullins did what most men do when they get caught. He said the words that always seemed to fit the occasion. What I do now? As he turned to walk into the bedroom, she followed him and grabbed his butt. "Nobody's hand goes here except mine, Mister," Jose said. "Yes, mam," he replied. It seemed that would have been the end of the butt grabbing, but Deidre had her agenda, as she was dead set on finding a way to get Mullins into her bed.

Chapter 7: Deidre's Obsession

When she got home, Dave was there waiting for her with carryout. "She walked in the door, and he asked, "How's my favorite girl?" "Your favorite girl is tired," she replied. With a serious look, he asked her if she was ok. "I know you, Deidre, and I can tell when something's wrong." "I said I was tired. " Can you please give it a rest?" she said grumpily. "Okay, listen, you've been in a bad mood since Mullins, and I returned from Alabama. So let's hear it," Dave insisted. "Maybe I just need some space Dave" she replied. "Space? You want space. I'll give you space," Dave shouted as he angrily walked out the door. Deidre walked over to the window and watched as Dave drove off. She knew she was being unfair to the man who had given her a place to stay when she was down on her luck. Her guilty conscience would not let her forget how she and Dave met. He was on assignment for a drug bust at a Topless dance bar in the Atlanta area. During the drug raid, he found this trembling young girl, frightened out of her mind, hiding in a closet. She had just got a job dancing, and the GBI raided the bar before she could get her first check. She was broke and homeless with no place to go. Dave took her to his one-bedroom apartment and gave her the bedroom while he took the couch. After a few weeks, they hit it off; the rest was history. And now, even though they had been together for a few years, it just wasn't enough to override the feelings that she was having for her new friend's husband. She knew there would be serious consequences if she got caught in her deeds, but she wanted that man so bad she could taste him. To hear his voice before she went to bed, she called to let them know she was home. Mullins answered the phone. "Hello," he said. "This is Deidre, and I was just letting you guys know that I made it home." And while she was expecting to hear more of Mullins' voice, to her surprise, Jose quickly took the phone from her husband and replied. "Okay, Deidre, thanks for calling a good night." Jose hung up the phone, and this time she turned to Mullins and said: "I'll take it from here." Jose had reached her boiling point, and Deidre was about to see the wrong side of an angry black woman. As for Dave, he was confused and had no idea why Deidre was acting so distant all of a sudden. She had become this strange person all of a sudden. As she lay across her bed, holding her hands to her face, she could smell Mullins cologne. She was satisfied clutching her pillow and imagining him there. Deidre had found herself uncontrollably obsessed with Dave's best friend and had no intentions of backing off. She wanted what Jose had and would not stop until she got what she wanted. Things could get very nasty between the Latin Lover and an Angry Black Woman who had plans to stand her ground. The smell of Mullins cologne pushed Deidre into a deep fantasy where she made love to her pillow and called out his name as if he were there.

Meanwhile, trouble was brewing in the good Senator's house in Mobile, Alabama. Attorney Gibbs had informed Senator Adams that Michael Browning had killed the hired shooter in Jackson, Georgia. So he decided to have a few drinks to ease his mind. His housekeeper, Sandy, knew from experience that the alcohol would cause an increase in his sexual appetite. Moreover, she knew he would come after her if she hung around long enough. So she asked his wife Amanda if she could have the rest of the day off. With her approval, she gathered her things and headed for the employee exit. But when she opened the door, Senator Adams was waiting with a drink in his hand. "Are you planning on leaving without having a drink with me, darling?" he asked. "I don't want any trouble, but if you must know, Mrs. Adams gave me the rest of the day off," Sandy replied. He then grabbed her by the arm, pushing her back into the employee change room, but to his surprise, Amanda walked in.

"What the hell do you think you're doing, Sam," she asked. "How can you give her the day off when she ain't done her damn job," he said with a guilty look. "And what job is that, Sam," Amanda asked. "Come along, Sandy; I'll walk you out." And I'll deal with you later, Mister," she added. Sandy looked at the Senator with a silent but stern face before walking out the door. She was engaged to a nice guy and could not wait for the day she could stop working for this evil man. There was nothing that the Senator could say or do to change what his wife had just witnessed. Finally, as the two women walked away, he shouted: "I know you don't think I was pushing up on that nigger maid of yours." But neither of the women paid him attention as they continued walking away. The Senator had no idea how close he was to his racist friends finding out that his wife and children were kindred to the people he so quickly referred to as nigger. Old folk used to say, "If you hate a race of people long enough, God will plant one in your garden." Jack Wallace was doing everything in his power to prevent anyone from ever knowing that his little girl had a black mother. But Jose was dead set on standing face to face with her long-lost daughter and saying, "I am your mother, and you are my daughter." One could only speculate what Amanda's reaction would be. And then there was another question of how the grandkids would react to finding out their grandmother was a black woman. The son Jody was more like his father, Senator Adams, but the daughter Jaelin was this lovely young girl who cared deeply for others. She always brought cold lemonade to the workers on hot summer days. The kids at school often tease her about her tanned skin, but Jaelin takes it as a compliment.

On the other hand, Jody had no problem using the "N" word. He was suspended once for calling a classmate a nigger. And when his mother told him that she would tell his father, his response was, "You think I might get a raise in my allowance?" His father had taught him to be a racist, and Jody had no problem letting anyone know he was a proud racist. Amanda was so afraid that one day someone would physically hurt him for his willingness to voice his racist opinion publicly. A racist sentiment shared by his father, who was soon to be Governor of the great state of Alabama.

However, Officers Mullins and Dave had other plans for the Senator. It was time to get back to work. Mullins called Dave from his car and was shocked to find out he was at Sarah's. "What the hell" Mullins reacted. "Just shut up and pick me up," Dave responded as he turned over for round two with a nice woman from the Browning Adoption Agency. He had somehow talked her into picking him up from his apartment after being rejected by his fiancé Deidre. When Mullins arrived at Sarah's house, Dave came out with a gym bag. "Man, what in the hell are you doing? Deidre is going to kill you," Mullins said. "Long story, partner," Dave replied as he laid his head back and closed his eyes. Mullins knew immediately that Dave was having trouble with Deidre, and he knew why. It was turning into something that could destroy the longtime friendship he and Dave had enjoyed for years. They were like brothers, and they always had each other's back. But Deidre was seriously challenging that friendship for her selfish reasons. And his longtime friend and partner was the victim. Telling Dave about Deidre's advances would be a bittersweet situation with the potential to destroy their friendship. Not to mention, one of the hardest things Mullins had ever had to do.

When they arrived at the station, Mullins woke Dave up. "Rise and shine, Casanova," Mullins said with a grin. "Don't even start that crap, man," Dave responded. When Mullins sat down at his desk, he noticed Jose had called. He immediately thought something was wrong because she had never phoned that early. Captain Mack was ready to go over the details of the Jack Wallace investigation, but Mullins had to check on Jose. "Be right there, Captain," he said as he dialed home for Jose. When she answered the phone, she said, "Deidre just called and wants to come for breakfast." "So when did you ever need my permission to have breakfast with Deidre," Mullins said jokingly. "Honey, I think she wants to tell me something, and I don't wanna hear. I love you, Robert, but I am scared of what she might say. So is there anything that I should know" Jose asked. "There is nothing that could ever draw me away from you and the kids, so just use your judgment when dealing with Deidre," Mullins replied. "My judgment is a left hook to the nose," Jose says in a low voice. "Yeah, love you too, and I heard that," Mullins replied as he shook his head before hanging up the phone.

So while Mullins, Dave, and the Captain went over the details of the Jack Wallace investigation, Jose was planning a lovely breakfast meeting with Deidre. She called her back and told her that breakfast would be OK. When she arrived, Jose was finishing up. "Oh my goodness, the food smells so good," Deidre said to set a friendly tone. But Jose was still debating whether to treat her like a friend or the thief she was. "So what shall we talk about," says Jose. Deidre just came straight out with a lie about Dave. "Dave walked out on me last night," she said. Her eyes were teary as if she were the victim. She wanted sympathy from Jose and Mullins so severely that she would sit there and make a statement that was sure to be checked for accuracy. "Well, if I had an extra man to lend you, I would kindly do so," Jose replied jokingly. "How can you make jokes at a time like this when everything is so upside down," Deidre said. She was demanding that Jose share her sadness, but she wasn't in the sharing mood. "Just relax, and he'll come around, but right now, we need to enjoy breakfast because I've worked too hard to waste it," Jose said as she sat down at the breakfast table. In conversation, Deidre asked Jose how things were going with Mullins. Jose paused for a moment. "Robert and I are doing just fine, and just for the record, I don't discuss my relationship with my man with anyone. And frankly, I don't care to hear your details," Jose added. "I didn't mean any harm," Deidre replied. "Well, it's time for me to get the boys up and running," says Jose with a severe look on her face. Deidre had a feeling that Jose was on to her plan. "I enjoyed the breakfast and the conversation. We should do it more often," Deidre said as Jose walked her to the door. When Deidre was inside her car, she opened her purse and pulled out a small medicine bottle. She gazed at the bottle with an evil eye. Rohypnol, the date rape drug, caused the victim to blackout with temporary memory loss. She planned to put it in Jose's coffee and trigger her amnesia, hoping the memory loss would last long enough for her to get closer to Mullins. Deidre's obsession was now with deadly intentions, as she waved goodbye to Jose while driving away. Jose had escaped Deidre's evil wrath, but it wasn't over by a long shot.

Meanwhile, Mullins and Dave were in conversation with the state police in Mobile, Alabama, concerning the kidnap charges against the man they'd come to know as Boss. They would be returning to Mobile in the last effort to bring Boss and his ring of criminals to justice. Captain Mack hoped Michael and JoAnn Browning would be willing to help, considering Boss's attempt on their lives. Mullins and Dave decided to take the rest of the day off and take care of the family business before leaving. Mullins went home to Jose, but Dave wasn't sure if he should go to Deidre or Sarah. After careful thought, he decided to go to Deidre's. When he arrived, he decided to knock instead of using his key.

When she came to the door, she opened it partially as if to say, "What do you want?" But Dave was determined to get some answers, so he walked past her and sat on the sofa. "Okay, Deidre, what's going on," he asked. "I thought you would give me some space," she said. "Listen, Deidre, I don't know what's going on with you, but if you're in trouble, I need to know," Dave replied. "There is nothing wrong with me. Now, will you please go" she screamed. Dave was shocked to see Deidre acting so irrationally. He got up and walked out of the door without looking back. Deidre closed the door behind him and sat down on the floor in tears. The tears were not because she'd lost Dave but rather because she was caught up in a love triangle with Jose and Mullins. Her heart was burning with desire for her best friend's husband while her longtime fiancé was driven back to Sarah Jenkins with an angry spirit. When Dave arrived at Sarah's, she opened the door and, without saying a word, led him to her bed. Here he was, this nice guy with a big heart, hurt and confused by Deidre's greed and selfishness. But Sarah wasted no time in attending to his wounded heart. As for Mullins, he and Jose were enjoying a lovely evening when the phone rang. It was Deidre crying and saying horrible things about how Dave treated her.

"Hold on. I'll get Jose on the phone," said Mullins as he handed the phone to Jose. "No, I need to talk to you so that you can talk to Dave and make him stop harassing me," Deidre said. She had no idea that he had already given the phone to Jose, who had taken all she could stand. "You listen to me, Deidre," she said. "My husband will not talk to Dave for you, and you will not call us today with your problems. Do I make myself clear?" Jose added in a calm voice. "Oh, my God. I am so sorry. Where are my manners" Deidre responded. "Goodbye, Deidre," Jose said as she hung up the phone. "Do you think Dave is having problems?" Mullins asked. "Shut up, Robert" Jose shouted. "You know what Deidre's doing with her damsel in distress act. And she will find out very soon what a mad black woman will do to protect her family." As it seemed, Jose had prepared to fight, but it's a different kind of fight when the opponent is mentally deranged.

The following day the dynamic duo, Officers Mullins and Dave, met at the station, all set to leave for Mobile, Alabama. "Okay, Captain. We're ready for takeoff," said Dave with a cheerful voice. "What the hell are you so cheery about this morning, champ," Mullins asked Dave. Dave smiled and grabbed his backpack as he headed for the car. "Damn, Captain, I need some of whatever he had," Mullins responded jokingly. "Just come back in one piece," said Captain Mack as he handed Officer Mullins the out-of-state search warrants for all of Jack Wallace's properties in Mobile, Alabama. When they arrived at the Atlanta Airport, a Jack Wallace informant had followed them there. He called Attorney Gibbs and informed him that the two GBI detectives were boarding their flight to Mobile, Alabama. Attorney Gibbs then called Boss to let him know that they were coming.

Meanwhile, Senator Adams was still trying to get revenge on Sandy, the black housekeeper. While she was cleaning his office, he told her that Amanda was on her way to pick the kids up from school. He also told her that she owed him an apology for leaving so soon on her last day of work. Sandy could smell the alcohol on his breath as he got closer. "Please, Senator Adams. I'm only here to do my job," she explained. But he would not take No for an answer. Instead, he grabbed her arms, forcing her against the wall as he angrily shoveled everything from the desk onto the floor.

She tried to get loose but was overpowered by this madman who was determined to have his way with her. With his hand clutched tightly around her neck Sandy fought with every ounce of her being while gasping for her last breath of fresh air. Her feet clawed endlessly against the hardwood floor until her strength was gone. She could only lay there pinned down on the desktop as he raped her helpless body. After he'd finished raping her, she asked with tears in her eyes, "Why did you do this to me?" He just looked at her and said: "Because I can." That's when Sandy told him she was going to the police and would not return to work again. But as she turned to leave the room, the Senator placed a coat hanger under her chin and choked her until she was dead. When her body fell to the floor, he realized what he had done and quickly called Attorney Gibbs to clean up another one of his many screwed-up situations. "Get over here right now," he said to Attorney Gibbs. The good Senator was not about to let anything hinder his chances for the Governor's Mansion. When Attorney Gibbs arrived, he saw the beautiful black woman lying on the floor.

"What in the hell have you done, Senator," he asked. "It's only a nigger, so shut up and get rid of it," he responded. "Get me a blanket and help me wrap her up," he said. When the two men wrapped Sandy's body up, the Senator told him to drag her out the back door so the neighbors wouldn't notice. Attorney Gibbs turned to the Senator and said, "Drag her your damn self. I'll bring the car around back." He could not believe the Senator's lack of compassion for human life. He had strangled the energy from this beautiful woman, who was soon to be happily married to her fiancé, Mike Bridges. And all the good senator could say was, "Drag it out the back way and get rid of it." To take the life of this innocent young black woman was evil, but to refer to her lifeless body as "It" was as demonic as the devil himself.

And after placing her body in the car's trunk, Gibbs called Boss and told him what his son-in-law had done. "That Bastard," Boss replied. "Meet me at the warehouse, and we'll get rid of the body," he added. When Attorney Gibbs arrived at the warehouse, Boss had his helpers transfer Sandy's body into a van. The plan was to place her in the trunk of her boyfriend's car after midnight. And the next day, the police would receive an anonymous call from someone sighting a black man putting what appeared to be a body wrapped in a blanket in the trunk of his car. Mike Bridges and Sandy were engaged to be married in the next couple of months. But now his hopes to marry the love of his life had been shattered. When the police pulled Mike over, they asked if they could look inside the trunk of his car. "I don't know what you're looking for in the trunk, but that's fine with me," he said. When the officers opened the trunk, they found Sandy's body wrapped in a blanket. They asked Mike to exit the vehicle and place his hands on it as they read his rights. "What's going on in my trunk," he asked. After being cuffed, they took him to the car's rear and pulled the blanket from Sandy's face. When he saw her, he fainted and fell to the ground. He was in total shock.

The officers looked at each other as if to say, "This was a total surprise to this guy." They made notes in the report of everything that happened from the time of the traffic stop until the boyfriend blacked out. "These notes just might come in handy if this guy has an alibi for the time of death," one officer said. When the ambulance arrived, the paramedics examined the boyfriend before transporting him to jail. He was in tears as he repeatedly said, "I didn't do it." As for the Senator, he was his usual self. When Amanda and the kids returned home, he asked if she'd brought him something to eat. "I'm starving, honey," he says.

When Officers Mullins and Dave arrived at the airport in Alabama, they were met by the SWATT team Captain and transported to the station for a briefing. While sitting in the break room, they overheard the two officers discussing the death of a woman Senator Adams employed. One of the officers mentioned that he was the son-in-law of jack Wallace. That caught Mullin's attention, so he and Dave introduced themselves and inquired about the death.

"We don't know much except her body was inside the boyfriend's trunk," one officer said. "And the strange thing is when he saw her dead and wrapped in the blanket, he fainted," the other officer said as he laughed it off. "May I ask how you came about looking inside his trunk?" Mullins said. "No, let me guess. It was an anonymous tip," he added. "How in the hell did you know," one officer asked as they casually walked away. Dave looked at Mullins and said, "Something tells me that this Jane Doe woman is somehow tied to Boss and his gang of criminals." The dynamic duo decided to share their scenario with the team Captain. They needed a starting point, and the deceased housekeeper, Sandy, seemed like an excellent place to start. They would soon learn that Jose's long-lost daughter was the dead woman's employer.

Chapter 8: Jose Has Doubts About Mullins

While Mullins and Dave leave no stone unturned in search of clues, Jose is home finding all sorts of house projects to keep her busy. Of course, Deidre is brainstorming ways to get close to her husband as soon as he returns. Finally, she decides to call, despite the rough-edged language used by Jose on their last breakfast date. "Hello, how's my good friend today," Deidre asked. "Your good friend is fine, and she thanks you for asking," Jose replies jokingly. "Well, I was hoping we could get together and maybe go to lunch," Deidre replied. Jose paused and responded with caution, "Why not?" She saw it as an opportunity for a woman-to-woman conversation that might end Deidre's obsession with her husband. "Then it's settled. I'll pick you up in about two hours," Deidre said as she looked down at the small medicine bottle. She was relentless, and at some point, she would put the Rohypnol in Jose's drink. She had gotten the date rape drugs from an old friend down on the strip where she worked as a prostitute and topless dancer. Her memory loss might be permanent if she successfully got Jose to take Rohypnol. This obsession for Mullins had taken a deadly turn, and Deidre had no boundaries. Jose decided to call Mullins and inform him of her intentions before going out with Deidre again. She was skeptical, considering how things turned out on the last outing when her son Levi got kidnapped. But Mullins thought it might be good for her and the kids to pick up where they left off and not live in fear. So it was settled, and the two ladies were ready to start their day. When Deidre arrived, it was exactly two hours, and that caused Jose to put up a red flag. She knew from experience that Deidre was never on time for anything. "You're on time?" Jose said as she walked up to the door. "Come on in; I'll just be a minute," she added. Deidre came in and began walking around the room as if she were planning a robbery. She was on her mental edge and a danger to everyone in her path. Finally, the two ladies and the kids went to South Lake Mall. When they got to the Mall exit, Jose asked if they could visit the small town of Jackson, Georgia, before going to the Mall. "Why would you ever want to go back there," Deidre asked with a curious look. "Sometimes it's good to remember where you came from," Jose replied. Deidre didn't know exactly how to take that comment, but she was determined not to remember where she'd come from and even more determined not to have to return.

When they arrived in Jackson, Jose pointed at the courthouse and said: "Right there is where I got my first taste of freedom." Deidre listened carefully as Jose talked about her experiences in the small town of Jackson, Georgia. While driving around the town square, Jose saw her sister Mildred and her husband, Wally. They were standing in front of Browning's Hardware & Gun Shop talking with Michael and JoAnn. "Oh my God, there she is," said Jose. "What are you talking about," Deidre asked. "Just pull back around and park in front of that hardware store," she said. When Deidre parked the car, Jose got out and walked over to her sister, whom she hadn't seen since her wedding day at Indian Springs State Park.

"Oh my God," Mildred said as she quickly ran over to hug her sister. "Where have you been, and why didn't you call me," Mildred said with teary eyes. "I am so sorry," Jose replied. The two sisters realized, at that moment, just how close they were. "Well, for starters, I want you to meet your nephews Levi and Bobby," says Jose. "Oh my, look at them. Girl, you will not leave this town again until I know exactly where you are," says Mildred as she reaches for a pen and paper from her purse. Michael and JoAnn were confused as the two sisters exchanged phone numbers and contact information. That's when Wally reminded them that she was his wife's sister.

"You guys remember a few years back when that black cop found the woman chained up at my father-in-law's place? The same guy that closed down the bowling alley and cost me my Park Ranger's job at Indian Springs State Park. Well, that's her, and she's married to that nigger." he said. Michael and JoAnn finally got closer to the woman at the center of their problems. "Okay, Wally, it was good talking to you," Michael said as he and JoAnn rushed back into the hardware store. JoAnn looked at Michael when they were inside and said: "She's found us, Michael." They both knew it was only a matter of time before the whole town would know about the illegal adoption and their affiliation with Jack Wallace. Jose had no idea she was standing a few feet away from the adoption agency owners who sold her daughter to Jack Wallace. When the two sisters ended their conversation, it was apparent that Wally was not a happy camper. But Mildred was so pleased that she called her sons, Terry and Gary, to tell them that she'd found Jose. They were delighted for their Mom because they knew how much she missed Jose. Mildred thought she would never see her sister again. But now, not only did she find her sister, but she also had nephews. So it was a good day for Jose and Mildred.

After the meeting, Deidre asked, "What in the hell was that all about?" "That my friend was my sister," Jose replied with a smile on her face. "Okay, off to the Mall," she added. Deidre did not know what to make of all she'd just witnessed because she had been told that Jose had no immediate family. Nevertheless, they were on their way to the South Lake Mall, and Jose had no idea she was in danger of losing her memory. She would not only lose the memory of Mullins and her children but the memory of her sister and her nephews would be lost as well. That small bottle of Rohypnol could destroy Jose's entire life. It would seem that Deidre would have second thoughts about putting the drug in Jose's drink. Especially after seeing how happy the two sisters were and hearing them make family plans. But no such luck because Deidre went into the restroom and broke open several Rohypnol capsules when they got to the mall. She emptied them into a smaller bottle and headed back to the food court, where she would rejoin her friend Jose. When she sat down, Jose told her to watch Bobby and Levi while she attended the ladies restroom. Deidre looked at the kids, and for a moment, she almost changed her mind. But her desire to get her grip on Mullins was overwhelming as she opened the medicine bottle and poured the Rohypnol into Jose's coke. As she stirred it with the straw, Levi asked if he could have some in his drink. She paused briefly before telling Levi, "No, this is for Mommy." Finally, Jose returned, and Levi asked her if he could have sugar in his coke. "You don't put sugar in coke, Levi," she said. "But Mom, you got some," Levi responded. "I said no, and if you ask again, I'll give you water," Jose responded jokingly. Levi wasn't taking any chances on losing his coke, so he shut up.

While drinking the coke, Jose mentioned that it tasted a little flat. "Mine does as well," Deidre replied. "Would you like another" she added. "No, I guess it's ok since you paid," Jose said jokingly. "Okay, guys, we're ready for window shopping, right?" Deidre asked. "Why not" Jose answered. As the ladies walked through the Mall, Jose asked Deidre if it would be okay if they rested for a while. Deidre knew that she had started to feel the effects of the Rohypnol. Suddenly Jose passed out on the Mall bench, and the kids began to cry for their mother., Deidre quickly called for help. "Can someone please call an ambulance" she shouted? After what seemed like an eternity, they arrived, and Deidre called Mullins, who was still in Alabama with Dave working on the kidnapping and murder case. When he heard the news, he and Dave went to the airport. "I'll stay here and follow up on the leads," Dave said as he hugged his partner, Officer Mullins. "Thanks, man," Mullins replied. "And please don't shoot anybody before we get a chance to interrogate them at least," Mullins added jokingly.

It was time for Officer Mullins to concentrate on his wife and kids. As for Jose, she was taken to the emergency room by ambulance while Deidre and the kids followed. It was almost unthinkable that Deidre could do such a thing. The kids sat silent until Levi asked: "Will my mommy be alright?" She couldn't even look into the child's face knowing what she'd done. When she reached the hospital emergency room, she told the desk clerk that she would be the point of contact for Jose Mullins. When the desk clerk opened Jose's file, she saw that Dr. Summers was her primary care physician. "We're in luck," said the registration clerk. "What do you mean," Deidre asked. "Well, it appears that her primary care physician is on call for the evening," she added. The clerk paged Dr. Summers, and she came immediately. Deidre told the doctor that she was in charge of her friend Jose and would make all the healthcare decisions. Dr. Price, refusing to acknowledge Deidre, turned her attention to the desk clerk. "Has anyone contacted Officer Mullins?" she asked. "No, we haven't," the clerk replied. "Then call him and let him know that his wife is in my custody," she added. "But doctor, for your information, I've already called Officer Mullins," said Deidre angrily. "And I'll be in the waiting room with the kids," she added. Dr. Summers asked, "Who are you?" I'm her best friend, Deidre, and these are her kids," she said. Dr. Summers thanked her for the information and reminded the clerk to inform her when Officer Mullins arrived. Deidre was angered even more that she was ignored by Dr. Summers.

Meanwhile, Officer Mullins contacted Captain Mack to inform him that while Dave was following up on leads in Mobile, he was going to the hospital to attend to Jose. "I hope she's okay," the Captain responded. He also told Mullins that he was closing out the murder case in Locust Grove concerning the parking lot shooting of Lil Rick at the Comfort Suite Hotel. Chief Wall had asked him to share the results of the Browning shooting, where they found a DNA match from the stranger in Michael Browning's driveway. It was quickly determined that he was, in fact, the shooter in Locust Grove, Georgia, as well as the kidnapper in Levi's case. It looked more like a cake walk for Jack Wallace by the minute. But Mullins and Dave were determined to tie him to the kidnapping and the murder of Lil Rick. Michael Browning and JoAnn had decided to work with Captain Mack since Jack Wallace (aka Boss) tried to assassinate them.

Finally, Officer Mullin's flight landed at the Atlanta Airport, where he rented a car and headed to the hospital. When he arrived, Deidre put on a show that would have won her an Oscar Award. She even had tears in her eyes as she held on to Officer Mullins like a damsel in distress. "Try and pull yourself together, Deidre. It's going to be okay," he said. "I'm going to find Jose, and we'll get to the bottom of it all," he explained. "I'll be right here with the kids," Deidre replied. "Please hurry," she added. Mullins turned and looked at Deidre again, thanking her for being such a good friend. He had no idea what this monster had done to his wife.

When he found Jose, Dr. Summers was with her. "I've ordered some blood work to try and determine the cause of the blackout," she explained. "And who is this woman so eager to be in charge of your wife's health care," she asked. "Oh yeah, that's Deidre. I don't know what Jose would've done without her," Mullins responded. "Yeah, right," Dr. Price replied. "Can I go in and see her?" Mullins asked. "Yes, please do, and if she awakes, call me immediately."

Mullins walked to her bedside and was reminded of the promises he'd made. The commitment to protect her from this evil world. His contract was never to let anyone hurt her again. Somehow he could feel her trying to speak to him, even with her eyes closed. He kissed her gently on her forehead and rubbed her cheeks. "I promise you, Jose, I'll be here waiting for you when you open your eyes." Mullins had once again found himself weeping for the love of his life. The nurse finally came in to tell him that Deidre was waiting to take the kids home. "She asked me to let you know that they were exhausted and tired from the day's events," she added. "Please tell her I'll be right out," Mullins said. He kissed his wife once more and told her he would be right back as soon as he made arrangements for the kids. At that time, Jose squeezed his hand slightly. Mullins started to yell for the nurse. "Nurse come quickly," he cried. When the nurse arrived, he told her that Jose had squeezed his hand. "That could have been a reflex," said the nurse to comfort him. But truth be told, Jose could hear their conversation but could not respond. Mullins walked away reluctantly as he looked back continuously. His instincts were telling him that Jose was trying to tell him something. When he reached the waiting area, Deidre asked if she was okay. "Do you think a brief visit would be ok? I want her to know I'll take care of the kids," Deidre explained. "I don't see why not," Mullins replied as he called for the nurse. He asked if Deidre could see Jose for a brief moment before leaving the hospital. "Okay, but just for a moment," she said. When Deidre entered the room, she walked over to Jose's bedside and whispered in a wicked voice, "I'll take good care of the hubby and the kids, but it's off to the crazy ward for you, sweetie."

Deidre was sure that Jose was unconscious. But what she didn't know was Jose could hear her every word. However, she could not respond, which was a temporary effect of the Rohypnol drug. Deidre was sure she'd have Mullins all to herself as soon as Jose was evaluated and admitted to the Learning Center. When she returned to the waiting room, she pretended to be torn and in tears. While Mullins consoled her, he told the nurse that Deidre was taking it hard because she and his wife were very close. When they left the room, one of the nurses looked at the other and said: "She's torn, alright." "Honey, the only thing she wants to tear is the sheets on his bed," the other nurse responded with a high five in agreement.

As Mullins loaded the kids in the car, Deidre offered to come along and help put the kids to bed. Mullins paused briefly but declined the offer. Instead, he thanked Deidre for all she'd done and drove off. When Deidre reached her car, she removed Rohypnol capsules from her purse. On her way home, she would get rid of the evidence by throwing them out of the window. Deidre knew it was only a matter of time before Mullins discovered that the date rape drug was in Jose's system. She wondered if it were possible to blame someone else. It was a dangerous game, but Deidre was in it to win it all.

The following day the phone rang, and it was Mildred, Jose's sister in Jackson, Georgia. She asked to speak to Jose, and Mullins told her that she'd been admitted to the hospital. Mildred told Mullins that she and Jose had been in conversation earlier and that she seemed to be okay. After a brief discussion, Mildred asked Mullins if he would meet her at the hospital. He told her he would meet her after making arrangements for the kids. He had serious reservations about calling Deidre but had no other choice. So he called her, and before asking her to keep the kids, she quickly volunteered to pick them up. But Mullins told her that he would drop them off at her house. She saw this as an opportunity to impress Mullins, so she prepared breakfast. When Mullins and the boys arrived, she wore a sexy red see-through nighty. The boys were still sleepy, so she put them back to bed for a while. After putting them to bed, she offered Mullins breakfast. "I can fix whatever you need." "No, I'm okay. I'll get something at the hospital," he replied. Then, she walked over to him seductively and said: "Anything you want or need, just ask me." Mullins was beginning to see why Jose reacted negatively toward her new friend Deidre. He could see through her nighty, enough to entice any man. But Mullins made it clear that his wife Jose was the only woman for him. "I appreciate you are caring for the boys, but that's as far as we go," he said as he left for the hospital. Deidre tried to conceal her anger, but Mullins could tell she wasn't thrilled with the rejection.

Meanwhile, his partner Dave was still in Mobile, Alabama, working on the Jack Wallace case. He called Mullins on the car phone and asked about Jose's condition. "How is she, partner," Dave asked. "Hanging in there," Mullins replied. "So, bring me up to date," he added. "Well, I'm on my way to the county jail to talk with the guy charged with murder," Dave said. "You mean the guy with the dead girlfriend in the trunk of his car," Mullins replied. "That would be the one," Dave responded. "Let me know how it turns out. I didn't like the smell test on that one," Mullins added. "Okay, will do," Dave said as he pulled into the parking lot at the Mobile County jail. When he walked into the prison, he asked the jailer to bring Mr. Mike Bridges to the interrogation room for some questions. When Mike walked in, he said, "I didn't do it." Dave asked Mike to sit down and listen. "Listen, fellow, I know you didn't do it, but I need your help finding the person who did," Dave explained. He put it all in perspective when Mike told Dave about Sandy's problems at the Senator's home. "When was the last time you saw your fiancé Sandy alive," Dave asked. "It was when she left for work that morning," Mike explained. "But when she didn't come home at her normal time, I got worried," he added. "And the next time you saw her was in the trunk of your car," Dave said in a guessing manner. "That's exactly what I'm saying," Mike replied. The puzzle pieces were now coming together, and it was time to visit Senator Adams. Sandy had been murdered, and her body was placed in her fiancé's trunk to shift the blame on him. A lot of questions were unanswered concerning Sandy's employers. Dave needed to know why the untimely death of a prominent family's housekeeper was so low-key. It seemed strange not in the investigation. He was almost sure of a cover-up of some sort. Especially since Senator Adams shared the exact attorney as Jack Wallace, it was becoming more evident that the Senator was connected to Jack Wallace in more ways than just a political arena.

As it seemed, the shooting at the Browning's home and the shootings at the Comfort Suites in Locust Grove were all connected to jack Wallace in some way. The Locust Grove police chief, Chief Wall, and Sheriff Wallace had also decided to keep their cases open and place Michael and JoAnn Browning under protective custody. Captain Mack assigned one of his undercover agents to stand guard at Browning Hardware & Gun Shop until the case was closed. JoAnn told Michael she had lost all trust in their old friend Jack (Boss) Wallace and that the illegal adoption in 1946 had become more trouble than it was worth. But it was nothing compared to the crisis unleashed if anyone ever found out that Jose's long-lost daughter was married to the prominent Senator Sam Adams of Alabama. JoAnn told Michael, "What if we just told everything and let the chips fall wherever they fall." "What in God's name are you talking about, woman? Do you want to spend the rest of your life behind bars or, even worse, buried six feet under? You tell me which it will be," Michael shouted. JoAnn turned to Michael in tears. "I am about to lose my mind Michael" she whispered as she lay her head on his chest. Michael could do nothing to console his wife except hold her tight and make her feel safe. "It will all be over soon, and we will be okay," Michael promised.

Meanwhile, Dave paid a visit to Senator Adam's home, and to his surprise, they had hired a new housekeeper already. "Hi, my name is Detective Dave Lamont, and I'm here to see the Senator," he said. "By the way, are you the housekeeper," he asked. "I am true. My name is Shanice, and I've only been here for two weeks." "What happened to the other housekeeper," Dave asked. "That will be all, Shanice," said the Senator as he rudely interrupted Dave's questionnaire. "Well, hello, sir," said Dave. "Do you make it a habit to interrogate the hired help without the employer's permission?" he asked. "Look, Senator, let's just cut through the crap. I'm investigating the death of many people who seem connected to you in one way or another," Dave explained. "This is the last place Sandy Broderick was seen alive. So if there's anything you can tell me, I'm all ears, Mister." Dave was losing his temper, and Officer Mullins was not around this time to reel him in. But the senator's wife, Amanda Adams, came to Dave's rescue. She went to the door to ask if she heard him correct about Sandy being deceased?" "Yes, Mam, you did," said Dave with a confused look. He was shocked that the Senator's wife didn't even know that her housekeeper was deceased but even more shocked that she looked like Jose's twin. It was a remarkable resemblance, but he kept quiet because he didn't want to jeopardize the investigation. So he continued to discuss the deceased with the senator's wife. "She was murdered a few days ago, and this was the last place she was seen alive," Dave replied.

After hearing about Sandy, Amanda covered her face and ran back into the house. "Well, I guess you're satisfied now that you've upset my wife," Senator Adams responded. "Sir, I do apologize for upsetting your wife and interrogating the new housekeeper, but the truth is, someone is dead, and I need some answers," said Dave as he turned and walked away. He immediately called Mullins to inform him that the Senator's wife was, without a doubt, Jose's daughter. Mullins was happy to hear the news, but he needed to see her with his own eyes before telling Jose. However, the report almost brought tears to his eyes when he thought of all the joy it would bring Jose.

Meanwhile, Mullins and Mildred waited patiently for the blood test results. Hopefully, it would reveal the reason for Jose's sudden blackout at the Mall. According to Deidre, it happened suddenly when she slumped over on the table and blacked out. Finally, Dr. Summers came over to talk with Officer Mullins. She hesitated for a moment before speaking because Mildred was sitting with him. "Where are my manners? Dr. Summers, this is Mildred, Jose's sister, and whatever you say to me is okay for her to hear," Mullins explained. "I didn't know she had a sister, but it's a pleasure to meet you finally," Dr. Summers said with a curious expression. "Anyway, I do have the results from the blood work, and it is positive as to what caused the blackout. Your wife tested positive for a date rape drug called Rohypnol," she explained. "But how did she get it in her system," Mullins asked. "I don't know, but the bad news is that it causes memory loss. And in Jose's case, the loss could be permanent," Dr. Summers added. "Oh, my God. Who was that woman she was with" asked Mildred.

"Oh no, that was her best friend, Deidre," Mullins replied. "Surely you guys don't think that Deidre could've done this," he said. "You find out, or I will, and it won't be pretty," Mildred said in anger. "Now, please take me to my sister," she insisted. When Mildred entered the room, she held Jose's hand. She could feel Jose slightly moving her fingers, so she asked for a moment alone. Out of respect, Dr. Summers and Mullins left the room. Mildred looked down at Jose and said: "They're gone now so that you can open your eyes." At that time, Jose opened her eyes and smiled at Mildred. "I knew you would come," she said with tears in her eyes. "She's trying to put me away and take my family," Jose whispered. "Who's trying to take your family" Mildred whispered back. "Deidre, the woman I introduced you to in Jackson," she responded. "Listen, they're going to send me to the Learning Center, and I'll let them. Please get my sons and keep them away from Deidre. As long as Deidre thinks I have no memory, I'm in no danger," Jose said. "But Jose, I'll help you fight," Mildred replied. "Please do it my way. Robert may not see through Deidre's evil tricks, so promise me you won't tell him I'm awake," Jose pleaded. "Okay, I will, and I love you, Jose," Mildred promised as she wiped her sister's tears. When she got to the door, she looked back a Jose and shook her head. "When this is over, you owe me big," said Mildred as she left the room. When she saw Mullins, she asked about the boys. "I'd like to see the boys again if you don't mind." "They are so adorable," she added. She planned to keep quiet until her nephews were safe and out of Deidre's reach. As for Jose, she would continue to fake her memory loss until she knew exactly who her enemies were. Her greatest fear was losing her family to her venomous friend Deidre. Time was not on her side, so she had to implement her plan immediately. She would give Deidre just enough rope to hang herself and catch her in the act of trying to finish what she had started. Jose knew that Deidre would try again because she could not afford for her to wake up and expose her evil deeds. If only Jose had listened to Levi at the food court when he asked for sugar in his coke. Then she would have known that Deidre put the substance in her drink. Sometimes kids say the silliest things, but it would have been better to listen this time.

When Mullins went by to pick up the boys, Deidre was again dressed provocatively. She wore a very short mini skirt with a low-cut tank top. As he walked in the door, she gave him a big hug as if she were greeting her husband. Dinner was ready, and a nice bottle of vintage wine was already on ice. But then Deidre's plan went wrong. Mildred had followed Mullins to her house and knocked on the door before Mullins could get comfortable. Deidre opened the door slightly. "May I help you?" she asked, hoping she would leave. But Mildred, the crafty one, saw Mullins inside and quickly jetted her way through the doorway. "Hey there, brother-in-law" and there are my little nephews," she added. Deidre's first thought was to grab Mildred by the neck and choke her down, but that would have ruined her plans. So she decided to take a more civilized approach and let Mildred know that this was not a good time to visit. She was determined not to let anyone mess up her dinner plans for her new family. Unfortunately, Deidre's obsession was overboard, and Mildred was pressing on her last nerve.

Suddenly, she remembered meeting Mildred in Jackson Square. "We weren't expecting any company," Deidre said. "Looks like you're expecting somebody for a lot more than dinner. I mean, with the wine and all," Mildred said as she looked at Deidre from head to toe. "But I just thought I'd follow Robert over and help with my nephews," she added. Deidre saw Mildred running interference, so she turned to Mullins. "Robert, I hope you don't mind that I took the liberty of preparing a little something for you and the boys, just in case you were hungry. Mullins looked at Mildred, standing in attack mode, and quickly turned Deidre down on her offer. "Well, I do appreciate it, Deidre. But I'll grab the boys and be on my way," he insisted. And again, thanks a bunch, he said as he took the boys to the car. Deidre had no idea what had just happened. She had worked all day preparing dinner and doing her nails and hair. She even had the foot massager plugged up in case Mullins wanted a foot massage. Yet, all she could say was, "That damn witch came and messed it up." When Mildred got to the car, loaded the kids, and whispered to Mullins. "I saved your ass that time so don't go back. Here's my number. I'll keep my nephews until my sister is well enough to tend to her own. And I won't take No for an answer," she added. "Ah, okay," Mullins replied. When he got in the car, he told Levi, "That's a mean Auntie, buddy," as he waved goodbye at Mildred.

While driving home, he called Captain Mack for an update on the case in Mobile, Alabama. "I think Dave's on to something, but how's your wife holding up," the Captain asked. 'She'll be fine as soon as Dr. Summers can get her transferred to Dr. Price at the Learning Center," Mullins responded. "Wow, that bad again, huh" Captain Mack replied. "Well, you take all the time you need. But the sooner you get back with Dave, the quicker we can tie this thing up," he added. Mullins knew he had to return to Mobile before Dave went off on a rampage and got them both kicked out of the state. He also knew that he couldn't tell the Captain just yet about the Senator's wife and her resemblance to Jose. So when he got home, he pulled out Mildred's phone number and called her. "Hello there. I didn't think I'd be calling you so early, but I need your help. "Where are you," he asked. "In your driveway on the Carphone, so open the door," she said. Mullins opened the door, and Mildred walked in and unpacked her things. "What are you doing," he asked. "Listen put the spare key on the table in case I need to get in from time to time, and you can go to work," she said. "Why are you standing there watching me? I got this, so go," she added. Mullins looked at Levi and Bobby, then turning his attention to Mildred, he said: "Are you sure?" Mildred shook her head and mumbled to Levi, "Is he deaf or what, Levi." "I heard that," Mullins said as he put the spare key on the table and left for the office. Mildred wasn't taking any chances on Deidre getting close to her nephews ever again. She was her sister's keeper and determined to make Deidre pay for what she'd done to Jose.

While driving back to GBI headquarters, Officer Mullins called Dave to let him know he was returning to Alabama as soon as he could get Jose admitted to the Learning Center. Dave had found out that the guy charged with the housekeeper's death had some compelling information. Mike Bridges planned to marry Sandy the following month. He told Dave that her employer was the last person to see his fiancé alive. "Tell you what. I'll fly out tomorrow as soon as possible," he said. "I'll be waiting," Dave replied. Mullins paused for a moment. He wanted to tell his partner Dave about the advancements from Deidre. But they were like brothers, and he didn't want to hurt his feelings unless necessary. "Okay, man, and If I see Deidre, I'll shout out for you," Mullins said. "Yeah, whatever, dude," Dave replied sadly. Mullins could tell something wasn't right, and he didn't like being in the middle. He and Dave had been partners and best friends for several years. When he reached the station, the Captain called him into his office. "Hey, let's take a ride to Jackson. We're meeting with your favorite people, the Brownings." "Okay, but what's the deal," Mullins asked. "The Brownings are turning states evidence against Jack Wallace, and you're taking the statements," he explained. "We're meeting them at the adoption agency," he added. When they arrived, the Brownings and Sheriff Wallace were already there.

"What in the hell is the Sheriff doing here? He's Boss's cousin, not to mention he's gone tell every detail of our discussion," Mullins said. "And that's why we've invited him to this fake meeting. When he thinks he has the details, he'll pass it on to Boss. Then we'll go to my office and rewrite the statements," he explained. "Old Cap still got game," Mullins said with a smile. They walked into the adoption agency, and Sarah Jenkins was at the front desk. Mullins could tell that she wanted to ask about Dave, so he asked Captain Mack to give him a minute to speak with her. And sure enough, her first words were, "How's Dave?" Mullins didn't want to do anything that might cause a final break up between Dave and Deidre, so he told Sarah that he was on the job that prevented him from calling home. But he promised her he would let him know she was thinking about him. Sarah's face lit up like a Christmas tree. It appeared Dave had made quite an impression before leaving for Alabama. And Sarah would be waiting for his return with open arms, which was more than he could expect from Deidre.

And now it was time for Mullins and Captain Mack to meet with the Brownings and Sheriff Wallace to discuss the possibility of amnesty and protective custody in exchange for their testimony against Jack Wallace. Michael Browning recorded a statement explaining their involvement but did not mention the illegal adoption of Jose's baby girl. Mullins knew that the Brownings were just as guilty as Jack Wallace, but he followed the Captain's plan. And just as they thought, Sheriff Wallace called Boss and told him there was no mention of the adoption in the Browning statement. But Boss was still highly concerned that they were now witnesses for the prosecution, and he wanted them eliminated. JoAnn was still frightened over the shooting in her driveway, but Michael showed no remorse. He was as mean and nasty as Boss, with no respect for human life besides his family. Before leaving Jackson, the Captain explained to the Brownings that law enforcement would set up around the hardware store and their home at all times. He reminded them that Jack Wallace was a very dangerous man with many resources and was sure to try and keep them from testifying in court. After the meeting, Mullins told the Captain that he needed to go to the hospital for Jose's transfer. And afterward, he would return to Mobile, Alabama, to join Dave in the Jack Wallace case. "Keep a close watch on that partner of yours and try not to let him shoot anybody this time around," said Captain Mack.

While en route to the hospital, Mullins received a phone call from Deidre. She wanted to know where the boys were and if she could help. Mullins tried to tell her about Jose's transfer, but he was uncertain how the drugs got into his wife's system. So he paused before telling her the boys were with their Aunt Mildred, and he was on his way to the hospital. "I would've been happy to keep them. It would have been what Jose wanted," she added angrily. "Well, Mildred is their Aunt, and I don't know how long I'll be gone, Deidre," Mullins replied. "It's not that I don't trust you. I just thought it might be good for the boys to get to know their Auntie," he added. Deidre became so angry that she hung up the phone while he was still talking.

Mullins was beginning to see a side of Deidre that he never knew existed. And Mildred's interfering with her plans caused her to lose control. She started breaking things and yelling at the walls. It was as if she had become this mad person who was angry at the world. Her obsession with her best friend's husband somehow led her down the path of no return. However, Mullin's primary concern was getting his wife the medical attention she desperately needed and keeping his family safe. When he arrived at the hospital, Dr. Summers was waiting for his signature on the transfer documents at the front desk. "Afternoon Dr. Summers. I was wondering if I could see Jose again before I sign her into the Learning Center. Who knows, she might wake up," he said jokingly. "That's quite alright," said Dr. Summers. "I'll be in my office whenever you're ready," she added. When Mullins walked into Jose's room, he leaned over and kissed her gently on her lips. "I am so sorry that I let this happen to you, and I promise I'll bring you back home safe and sound. And don't worry about the boys because your crazy sister Mildred has them," he said. Jose wanted so badly to open her eyes, but she had to be sure that Deidre was working alone when she was drugged. Just the possibility of her husband being involved was tearing her apart inside. But the only sure way to trap Deidre was to remain unconscious. Before leaving her bedside, he leaned over and gently kissed her lips. And as soon as he left the room, she opened her eyes. Tears were streaming down her face. Her heart was broken because of the uncertainty. She knew that Mullins loved her dearly, but she also knew that he was constantly defending Deidre's actions. And there was no room for error in her plan.

Meanwhile, Mullins returned to Dr. Summer's office and signed the transfer documents for Jose's transport to the Learning Center, where she would be further evaluated. Jose knew her greatest challenge would be convincing Dr. Price to keep her secret. It was inevitable that the doctor would examine her pupils and find that she was awake. When they arrived at the Learning Center, Mullins followed Jose, holding her hand every step and hoping she would open her eyes and say, "Take me home." But again, he found himself sitting in Dr. Price's office, asking her to perform yet another miracle. "Well, here we are again," Dr. Price said. "I've spoken with Dr. Summers, and she's informed me of the drug found in Jose's system." "And I will find out who put it there," Mullins replied. "All I need you to do is protect her while she's here and help her recover," he added with tears in his eyes. Even though Jose wondered why Mullins trusted Deidre so much, she not once doubted his love for her. She knew without a doubt no one in the world loved her more. On his way out, Mullins stopped by Jose's room to tell her that he was returning to Mobile, Alabama, to finish what he'd started. He leaned over and told her to hang in there. "I'll be back for you, Jose, and I'll find out who did this to you," he said. He wanted to tell her "I've found your daughter" so badly but didn't want to excite her emotions. When he left the room, she listened to the door close and again opened her eyes.

When Mullins arrived at the Atlanta airport, he called Mildred to tell her that Jose had been transferred to the Learning Center and that she was the only person authorized to visit. "Tell the boys I'll be back as soon as possible. And thank you so much for taking care of them," he said. She paused for a moment to look down at little Bobby and Levi, and then with teary eyes, she said: "We'll have that cookout waiting when you get back." Mildred enjoyed her time with her nephews, but her husband, Wally, was not as thrilled with the idea. "So, how long are you planning on keeping them," Wally asked. "As long as I want," Mildred said as she walked away. It was almost certain that Wally would have a problem with black kids in the home. Still, Mildred would prevail, especially since she'd inherited all of Kyle's properties, including the family residence. "I'm thinking about giving my sister Jose some land here in Butts County," she said. "Might even become sisterly neighbors," she shouted. "You can't be serious," Wally replied. "Not only am I serious, but it's the right thing to do," said Mildred. Wally slammed the door in anger while Mildred turned to Levi and said. "Who wants cake and ice cream?" She knew how to rattle Wally's cage and did it with great pleasure. And nothing would make her life more complete than to have her only sister living on the Kyle property. The two sisters had become closer than Wally could ever imagine.

Chapter 9: Jose Trap for Deidre

Finally, Mullins is back in Mobile, Alabama, ready for Dave to bring him up to date. "Why don't we just start by paying the good Senator another visit" Dave suggested. The dynamic duo agreed to return to Senator Adam's home to try and rattle his cage so that he would volunteer information. Igniting his anger seemed to cause somehow him to talk more than usual. When they arrived, his wife Amanda came out to meet them. "May I help you?" she asked. Mullins just stood there as if he'd seen a ghost. "Told you, dude, this is some weird shit," Dave said? Suddenly the Senator came out of the house. "Amanda, come inside now," he shouted. "Why are you guys here," he asked in anger. "We're investigating the death of your housekeeper," Dave answered. As Mullins came closer, Senator Adams recognized him from the photos in the package that the hired shooter had obtained. It was a photo of little Levi's father, but even worse; this man was married to his wife's biological mother. And now his only hope was that Mullins would leave and never come back.

"Leave now unless you have a warrant," he said. "Let's go, Dave. Sorry to bother you, sir," Mullins said. "What in the hell kind of talk is that," Dave asked. "I said let's go, Dave," Mullins said as he hurried to the car. "You better have a damn good explanation for turning tail and running," Dave said. "You're right about his wife," said Mullins. "She looks like Jose's sister. If my eyes were closed, I wouldn't be able to tell the difference in the voices," he added. "That's what I'm saying, dude. So why are we leaving" Dave replied. "I think Senator Adams recognized me," Mullins said. "Told you, man, she looks just like her," Dave said. "Unless my eyes and ears for fooling me, dude, hell yeah," Mullins replied. "I'd recognize that voice anywhere, and I'm telling you, it was Jose's voice," he added. "Then let's go back and get her," said Dave. "Not just yet. We need to take this real slow," Mullins said. "How about we talk about it over dinner, dude" Dave replied. While Dave and Mullins enjoyed a nice dinner, Senator Adams was on the phone with Jack Wallace to tell him that the nosey Cop from Georgia was on his daughter's doorstep. As soon as Boss heard the news, he knew Mullins had recognized Amanda. He knew it was only a matter of time before his wife, Jose, would stand face-to-face with his adopted daughter. And the very thought angered him even more. "These boys just bought themselves a ticket straight to hell," Boss replied angrily. "That's one thing we can agree on," the Senator replied. "Send Amanda and the kids on a vacation, son," Boss said. Both men knew that Mullins had recognized the resemblance between Jose and Amanda. "Okay, Boss, I'll keep Amanda and the kids away for a while, but those

GBI guys from Georgia are here because of you," he said. "Just let me handle it, and you stay out of my way," said Boss. "And one more thing. Don't play house with the damn housekeeper while my daughter is gone. And I damn well mean it," he added. Of course, the perverted senator was sure to make sexual advances toward the new housekeeper's first chance he got. But he knew the vacation was the only way for Amanda to avoid Mullins, so he convinced her that a nice trip to Aruba was just what they needed. He told her he would have to join them after his business meeting. But he didn't know that Officer Mullins and his partner Dave were staked out at his residence all night.

When the Limo pulled around the following day to load the family for the airport, they were watching. "Gotcha," Mullins said. "Looks like we spooked them into going on a trip," Dave replied. They watched as the wife and kids got into the Limo while the good Senator went back into the house. They followed the senator's family to the airport and inside the terminal, waiting and watching until they boarded a flight to Aruba. "I'm beginning to think he just doesn't want us talking to his wife," Mullins said. "Well, I think we should call the Captain for tickets to Aruba," Dave said jokingly. "You're the right partner. We follow the leads wherever they take us," Mullins said. But when they called Captain Mack, it was a monumental error. "Do you guys think I'm sending you to Aruba?" Mack said. "Just hear me out, Captain," Mullins replied. "You won't believe this, but I just saw Senator Adam's wife, and she looks and sounds exactly like Jose's twin sister." "Are you saying what I think you're saying?" Captain Mack asked.

"That's exactly what I'm saying, but I'm not sure how he fits in with Jack Wallace," Mullins added. Even though it would have been nice to know more about the senator's wife, Captain Mack did not have the authority to send his guys abroad to Aruba. He would need an international warrant as well as FBI involvement. So they were instructed to stay with the investigation of Jack Wallace and find out how close he was to Senator Adams. Now, things were moving at warp speed, and Mullins had little time to decide what he would tell Jose. There was no doubt that she would set up camp at Senator Adam's doorstep if she thought for a moment that her daughter was anywhere on the property. She was lying in her bed at the Learning Center, thinking of holding her child again. Each time the door opened, she would close her eyes and hope that it was Mullins with the news that he'd found her. Not one minute had passed without her trying to imagine her facial features. She would often daydream of simple things such as combing her hair or getting dressed for school. Jose had gone through so much in her life; finally, holding her daughter would be the ultimate achievement. She had total confidence that Mullins would leave no stone unturned in his search. As for Mildred, she had a bittersweet feeling about Jose finding her daughter because she was ashamed of the past and what her father, Mr. Kyle, had done. She knew from experience what it felt like to see someone for the first time and to stand face to face with a stranger and see a mirror reflection of yourself. It happened to her a few years earlier in the Butts County Courtroom when she first laid eyes on her biological sister Jose. Mildred would never forget asking her father, "Daddy, what have you done?" And now she could meet another sister who would also be her niece. The thought constantly ran through Mildred's mind. It seemed almost inevitable that the three ladies, Jose, Mildred, and Amanda, would one day sit for coffee in the small town of Jackson, Georgia. One could only imagine the conversation sparked if Jose found Amanda. One thing for sure was that all three women had a striking resemblance that could prove deadly consequences for the GBI duo from Georgia.

And speaking of deadly consequences, as Mullins and Dave were driving back to their hotel, they noticed a blue Dodge truck following from when they left the airport. He turned off the freeway to avoid gunfire in heavy traffic, but the truck continued to follow. "Okay, Dave, get ready for some action. I think we finally got someone's attention." Mullins said. Then all of a sudden, the truck rammed the rear end of the rental car. Dave pulled out his service revolver while Mullins pulled over to the curb, but the truck didn't stop. So they gave chase, and the passenger leaned out of the window and fired shots as they got closer. "What in the hell are they doing," Mullins said. "I don't know, but I've been waiting for a reason to shoot somebody in Alabama," Dave replied as he returned fire.

"Stay close and hold it sturdy," Dave added as he aimed, striking the tire on the right rear side. When the tire blew, the truck started to weave before hitting the curb and flipping over. Officer Mullins and Dave pulled over to observe the wreckage. They didn't know if the passengers were dead or alive, but they knew firearms were in the vehicle. Approaching the truck with caution, they found the occupants disoriented but alive, so they secured the weapons and cuffed them. Dave calls for an ambulance and local backup. It was apparent that Senator Adams had made a call to some nasty people, but there were still several dots to be connected. It seemed more likely that he was somehow involved in the murder of Sandy, the housekeeper, but the evidence was yet to be uncovered. When the ambulance arrived, the two guys were treated for minor injuries and transported to jail. Mullins and Dave hoped to get information from them before they were released on bail. They knew that if these guys were connected to the Senator, the time for interrogation would be minimum.

They took turns interrogating each of the guys for at least two hours, and they were rock solid and refused to talk. Finally, Officer Mullins got this long-shot idea and told each guy that the Senator wanted them both silenced. He told them someone on the inside had already been hired and that they wouldn't last until daybreak. "So tell me, big guy, how it feels to be hired by some rich politician to do his dirt. Then when it goes sour, he calls in and puts a jailhouse hit on you," Mullins asked. At the same time, Dave told the other guy the same story. And when they told each guy that the other had snitched to save his own life, they decided to talk. "Well, all I know is this lawyer named Attorney Gibbs hired us to scare Y'all up a bit," said one of the guys. When asked how much he was paid, he said they weren't sure, but it would be after the job was finished. Officer Mullins knew then that he had to find a way to keep these guys apart and isolated from the population. But there was another problem. Attorney Gibbs and Jack Wallace had long arms that reached far inside the police force, and there was no way to know who was actually on the payroll. And just like clockwork, both guys made bail early the following day. Officer Mullins could not believe that a Judge would release anyone who had just fired shots at police officers. Not to mention the other charges filed. Dave went to the jail clerk to see who signed their bail bond, and it was none other than Attorney Gibbs. "I don't think we'll ever see those guys again," said Dave as he shook his head in disgust. "You got that right," Mullins replied.

The following day Mildred decided to visit Jose at the Learning Center. She and Mullins were the only persons authorized to see her besides Dr. Price's medical staff and Dr. Summers. Before going into the room, she had a short conference with Dr. Price. She told Mildred that it would likely be a slow process and that bringing the kids around for visitation was never a good idea. Even though Levi wanted to visit his mother, Mildred had left them both at the daycare in Jackson with a close friend. "I was wondering if someone was watching her door at all times to ensure her safety," Mildred asked. "Well, the doors on the secure hall are protected by combination locks," Dr. Price explained. "Come with me, and I'll show you how it works," she added. When they reached Jose's room, the doctor punched in the 6-digit code and opened the door. "There is also a flashing red light that comes on both here, and at the nurse's station each time these doors are opened, and it continues to flash until that person leaves the room," she explained. Mildred entered the room and walked over to her sister Jose. She turned to the doctor and asked if she could have time alone with her. "Not a problem," said Dr. Price. "I'll meet you back at my office when you're done with your visit," she added before leaving the room. Mildred took Jose's hand, and she opened her eyes. "I have the boys with me, and they're doing fine," she said. "Thanks for everything you're doing," Jose replied. "It won't be long before Dr. Price figures out that I'm awake, so I need you to allow Deidre visitation rights," she added. "Did your brain go on vacation, or did you just forget that she's the reason you're here" Mildred whispered. "Listen, just as sure as she's a coward, she will say everything to me that she's afraid to say to my face," Jose replied. "She added; she won't know that I'll be recording every word underneath the covers," she added. "All I have to do is pretend asleep and helpless." "I don't know Jose. She pretty whacked out," Mildred said with reluctance. "Do this for me and bring me a small tape recorder. I can handle her," Jose replied. "Okay, I'll do it, but you got two weeks tops, and I'm taking you home because your sons need you," Mildred said with teary eyes as she kissed Jose on the forehead. "Don't forget to bring the recorder?" Jose said, smiling at Mildred. When she left the room, her first stop was the nurse's station to observe how the flashing red light worked. And just like the doctor said, the nurse would terminate the visit when the visitor left the room by turning the light off. Mildred felt much better about her sister's safety during her stay at the Learning Center.

And now, it was time for her to convince Dr. Price to allow Deidre to be added to Jose's visitation list. "I don't know if you're aware, but according to Dr. Summers, this Deidre woman is suspected of putting the drug in Jose's drink," she added. "And I'm going to need approval from her husband even to consider it," said Dr. Price. "Maybe you're the right doctor. Why don't we discuss it when Officer Mullins returns" Mildred said. She knew immediately that she didn't have time to wait for Mullins to return from his trip. So she decided to invite Deidre along with her to the Learning Center and sign her in. It seemed even safer because she would help Jose if anything went wrong. So she called Deidre to set up the visit and gladly accepted. "Thank you so much for inviting me. I was wondering when you guys were ever gonna call me," Deidre said.

"Yeah, I know you guys are such good friends, and I know Jose would want you to come," Mildred replied. "So when is your next visit," Deidre asked. "Day after tomorrow at 10 am," Mildred answered. "Then it's a date for Thursday at 10 am. I will meet you there," Deidre replied. The thought of getting one more chance at finishing Jose was a dream come true. But little did she know that Mildred would be watching from the security monitor at the nurse's desk. Levi ran to her as if she were Santa Claus when she picked him up. Mildred was spoiling her nephews at every turn with treats and toys. But while enjoying every minute of being the good Auntie, her sister's safety was her priority.

The following day during the 6 am rounds, Dr. Price noticed additional brain activity on Jose's charts. So she opened her eyes lids and shined the light on her pupils. She knew that Jose was awake but didn't know why she was pretending to be asleep. So she decided to play along and give her a couple days to wake up. However, she immediately went back to her office and called her husband. "Good Morning Officer Mullins. I'm sorry to call so early, but I have great news," she said. "Good news is exactly what I need," Mullins replied. "Well, the good news is that your wife is awake, and the bad news is that she's pretending to be asleep," she said. "What do you mean, doctor," Mullins asked. "I think we need to continue this conversation in my office," she said. "That's all I need to hear. I can be home by tomorrow night and in your office early Thursday morning," he said. "Okay, I'll see you then," said Dr. Price. His first thought was to call Mildred, but he surprised her and the kids after visiting with Jose.

At breakfast, he couldn't wait to tell Dave that Jose was awake. "That's great news, man. I told you she would be okay," Dave replied. "You know I'll be flying out sometime this afternoon, so can we please wait until I get back before going back to Senator Adam's house," he asked. "Yeah, man. I got another interview with Sandy's boyfriend, Mike, today. I'm hoping he can tell me a little more about Senator Adam's family," he said. "Yeah, maybe we can figure out who put her body in the trunk of his car," Mullins replied as they left for the station. While driving through downtown Mobile, Mullins decided to ask Dave about Deidre. "So, how's it going with Deidre these days? I haven't heard you talk about her since we got here." "Man, she asked me for some space, and I gave her all she could handle," Dave replied. "Meaning what partner," Mullins asked. "Meaning she's acting funny as hell, and I ain't trying to figure it out," he replied angrily. Dave's answer gave Mullins reason to worry that Deidre might have been responsible for the Rohypnol in Jose's system. However, he didn't want to accuse his partner's girlfriend without some concrete evidence.

That would be a messy situation if it turned out to be accidental. When they arrived at the station, they both checked messages from Captain Mack. Mullins decided not to tell the Captain about the drug found in Jose's system until he was back on Georgia soil. While Dave prepared for Mike Bridge's interview, Mullins called the airport and scheduled his flight back to Atlanta. His early return could punch holes in Mildred and Jose's plan to catch Deidre at her tricks, especially if Dave had decided to share the good news with Deidre.

Mullins was able to schedule a flight from Alabama to Atlanta departing at 11 pm and arriving at 2 am Thursday. It would give him a few hours to sleep before going to the Learning Center. As much as he would've liked to see Levi and Bobby, he knew that he wouldn't get much sleep if he picked them up at 2 am, not to mention he didn't want to make Aunt Mildred angry with even the thought of waking them that early. So he decided to arrive at the Learning Center around 10 am. When he arrived, he met with Dr. Price, and they went to the secure ward to visit Jose. To both their surprise, Mildred was already there, and Jose's plan was already in action.

"Why are you all gathered around the monitor," Dr. Price asked with an angry look on her face. "This monitor says room number 320. Why are you guys watching Jose's room monitor" Mullins asked. "I asked the nurse if I could observe the monitor while Deidre visited Jose," Mildred answered. "Who in the hell authorized the visit" Mullins shouted as he ran down the hallway to Jose's room. Mildred tried to stop him, but it was too late. Jose's plan was about to be ruined.

Meanwhile, Deidre had just entered the room. She called Jose's name several times to see if she was still asleep. When she didn't answer, she grabbed Jose's hand to observe the IV inlet valve. She reached inside her purse with the other hand and said: "This time, I'll give you enough to keep your sleep forever." Jose pretended to be asleep and heard every word Deidre noted but did not have the recorder activated. And just as Deidre was about to pull out the syringe, Officer Mullins burst into the room. "What are you doing here, Deidre," he asked. "And why is your hand in your purse?" Deidre had to think fast, so she pulled out a small bottle of hand lotion. "Her hands are so rough, and I wanted to rub them with hand lotion," she responded. Deidre pretended to be so hurt that she burst into tears and ran out of the room. "Come back, Deidre. I didn't mean it that way," Mullins shouted as he followed her down the hallway. But Deidre kept running past the nurse's station to her car. Jose wanted to open her eyes and tell Mullins what she'd just heard Deidre say, but it would have blown her cover. Mildred and Dr. Price met Mullins in the hallway and asked him what had happened. He told them that he walked into the room and saw Deidre with one hand in her purse while holding Jose's hand with the other. "I think I may have wrongfully accused her of doing something underhanded, and I am so sorry," he said. "Someone should go after her," he added. "Let her go, Mullins. She's not as innocent as she seems," said Mildred. "Well, if you knew her, then you would know that she's taking this whole thing very hard,"

Mullins said as he headed back to Jose's room. "Not as hard as she would like to take it," Mildred said to the nurse. "I know that's a right child with his fine self," the nurse responded jokingly.

As for Deidre, she wasted no time leaving the Learning Center. She pulled over at a gas station while driving a few miles away. She had the evilest look in her eyes as she opened her purse, and there it was. A syringe needle that was meant for Jose. As it appeared, Officer Mullin's instincts were right. And to question Deidre's hand in her purse may have saved Jose's life because the intent was to inject her IV with another hefty dose of Rohypnol. Only this time, the date rape drug would have sent Jose twirling into a permanent coma. Mullins thought Jose was asleep, so he decided to pick up his sons while Mildred finished her sisterly visit. "Why don't I just pick the boys up from the daycare, and you can spend more time with Jose," Mullins said. "The best thing I've heard from you all day, brother-in-law," Mildred replied with a smile. "Listen, why don't you call me Robert," he said. "With your mean self," he added as he walked away laughing. "I heard that big guy," says Mildred jokingly. When the room was all clear, Jose opened her eyes, and the two stared at each other. Then finally, Mildred spoke. "This cat and mouse game has to end, Jose." She looked at Mildred with teary eyes and said: "I heard every word." "What do you mean you heard every word," Mildred asked. Jose repeated, "She thought I was asleep and told me she would give me a larger dose this time. I couldn't believe she was saying these horrible words," Jose added. "Just tell me you recorded it all because I'm ready to lock that monster up." Jose handed Mildred the recorder with a sad face. "I forgot to press record," she said. "Well, just for the record, there are safer ways to find out if people can be trusted," Mildred said. She kissed Jose on the forehead. "I'll be awake tomorrow morning when Dr. Price makes her rounds," Jose said. "Hopefully, she will let me come home," she added. "Honey, this place reminds me of Friday the 13th," Mildred replied as she left the room. As for Jose, she didn't have to pretend to be asleep anymore; it was like a breath of fresh air. However, she would still have to deal with the issue of Deidre and the Rohypnol drug found in her system. It would be almost impossible to prove that she did it, but at least she knew who her enemies were. If only she had used the recording device. As for Mullins, he didn't think Deidre was capable, but his instinct caused him to at least question her actions. Only time would tell as to whether he would fall into her trap.

On the way to pick up the kids, Mullins decided to stop by Deidre's place and apologize for not trusting her at the Learning Center. When she saw him pull into her driveway, she hurried to the bedroom to change into a sexy nightgown. When he rang the doorbell, she quickly opened the door. Mullins saw that she was partially dressed and told her he only came by to check on her. "I just wanted to apologize for how I acted at the Learning Center," he said while standing at the front entrance. "Please come in," she said. "No, I can see that you're resting, so maybe another time," Mullins responded. Deidre could see that he wouldn't come inside, so she made a desperate move. She broke into tears and fell to the floor in the doorway with the door still open. She knew that he couldn't just walk away and leave her lying there. "Oh my God,

Deidre," he said. "Are you okay?" he asked as he quickly entered and helped her onto the sofa. "I've been feeling a little bit weak for a couple of days," she said tremblingly. "Would you like me to call Dave?" he asked. "No, please don't. Dave and I aren't together anymore. Didn't he tell you" she asked. "Well, let's not talk about that right now. Can you make it to the bed" he asked. "Maybe, I mean, I can try," she mumbled in a weak voice. "Okay, here we go," Mullins said as he picked her up and carried her to the bedroom. When Deidre got to the bed, she turned to Mullins and shoved her tongue in his mouth while attempting to pull him over her. But as tempting as it was, he stopped her in her tracks. "There's only one woman for me, Deidre. And if I did anything to lead you on, I am truly sorry," Mullins explained.

"Oh, silly me. I'm the one who should be sorry. I get so lonely since Dave dumped me," she said, tears welling in her eyes. "But I'll be okay," she added. "Listen, again, I'm sorry, and don't worry about me saying anything to Jose or Dave," he replied as he left the house. As he walked quickly to his car, all he thought was how close he'd just come to falling in Deidre's web. He was beginning to see precisely why Jose had trust issues with her. He was also beginning to understand why Dave was pulling away from her. She says Dave dumped her, but Dave said that she asked for space. Someone was lying, and it was apparent that someone was Deidre.

Nevertheless, Mullins knew that all hell would break loose if Jose or Dave ever found out about Deidre's seductive attempt to lure him into bed. And he knew that it would be even worse if they found out and he wasn't the one to tell them. It would certainly make him appear just as guilty. The strange thing with men is that they always feel that the woman is disloyal when she doesn't tell. But when the shoe is on the other foot, it's better to keep things quiet and let it play out. Mullins knew this could poison his marriage and his friendship with Dave. It was an old saying "Truth Untold is a Lie waiting to Unfold." Mullins had promised Jose he would never lie to her, but the deception was already beginning to feel like a lie. Deidre had planted her venom in his heart, and there were only two choices. He could tell it right away and let the chips fall where they fall or hold on to it and risk losing everything. Jose was already angry and feeling betrayed by the trust he had shown for Deidre at the Learning Center. And this incident, if handled wrong, could be the straw that breaks the camel's back.

When he arrived at the daycare, his sons Levi and Bobby were excited to see him. Mullins held tight to Levi's hand as he pushed Little Bobby in the stroller. He wasn't taking any chances on another snatch-and-grab surprise while loading them in the car. "Now, who wants pizza," says Mullins as they head for the nearest pizza joint. The boys were happy, but he was sad that his wife was still at the Learning Center alone. So after the pizza joint, he decided to go with his gut and carry his sons to see their mother, even though Jose had asked that he not bring them there. "Okay, who wants to go see Mommy," he asked. Levi looked up at his Dad and said: "But we can't because she's sick." "Well then, maybe she needs us to come and make her well," he replied. "Dad," Levis asked as his face lit up with excitement. So the trio headed for the Learning Center. When they got there, Dr. Price had left for the day. Mullins and his two sons walked up to the nurse's desk and asked to be signed in. The nurse looked at Mullin's sad face and said: "Officer Mullins, you are aware that kids under the age of 16 are not allowed in the secure hallways." "But I'm gone take a coffee break. I should be back in maybe 30 minutes". The nurse smiled and said, "Say hello to me," as she walked away from the desk. Mullins noticed a fresh cup of coffee on the desk. He touched the cup, and when he saw it was still hot, he knew she was allowing him enough time for the boys to visit their mother. So the trio headed to Jose's room, where Mullins punched in the code and entered.

When Jose heard Levi yell Mommy, she quickly opened her eyes and sat in bed, forgetting about her illness. "Well, well, well. So much for Sleeping Beauty," Mullins said while smiling at his happily reunited family. "I'll go get your clothes. I'm taking my wife home right now," he said, tears welling in his eyes. He walked over to her bedside and hugged her. "I love you, Robert," she said. "And I love you, Mrs. Mullins," he replied. "I am so sorry for letting you down," Jose added. But before she could say another word, Mullins put his finger gently over her lips. "You don't need to apologize for things that are not your fault, and don't you ever lose your faith in me because I love you more than life itself," he said. All Jose could do was smile and shake her head. "I feel so loved right now, so go find my clothes," she said jokingly. "I will be right back. Come along before I lose my badge for slipping kids on the secure hallway. And don't you go back to sleep, woman," he said as he left the room.

When he got to the desk, the nurse was watching the monitor. "You guys got me crying and messing up my makeup. And makeup is expensive," she said as she handed Mullins Jose's clothes. "And don't worry, I've already called Dr. Price, and she's on her way here as we speak. So go get your wife, man," she said. Levi and Bobby waited with the nurse while Mullins hurried back down the hallway with Jose's clothes.

When Mullins entered the room with Jose's clothes, her face lit up like a Christmas tree. When she got dressed and walked to the nurse's station for checkout, Dr. Price arrived. "Did you guys think I would let you all take my favorite patient without saying goodbye?" "Okay young lady, I need you to come into my office to get a proper release," Dr. Price said.

When she got into the office, she told Jose that she knew she'd been awake for a couple of days. "Oh my God, why didn't you tell me," Jose said. "Now, why would I tell you something that you already knew? Just say you'll be careful with selecting friends in the future because someone close to you put a drug called Rohypnol in your food or drink." "Thanks again, Dr. Price," Jose said as she left the office to join her family. As they walked out of the door, the nurse looked at Dr. Price and said: "Now that's what true love is right there, and I'm gone get mine one day." "Yeah, right," said Dr. Price. "Just like the last one you got." "Why are you all up in my business Dr. Price," the nurse said jokingly. "Just reminding you of your Boaz, who left town without a trace," she added. The two women had worked together for years. They'd become best friends over time. Two things they both had in common were neither of them had a husband, and they were both committed to helping others find their way out of the darkest places of the mind. In addition, Dr. Price could feel her patient's pain. A unique quality that most Psychiatrists lack.

When Mullins got home, he called Mildred to tell her that her sister was home and doing fine. But she insisted on speaking to Jose. "Okay, you can talk but not all night because we just got her back," Mullins said jokingly. "I mean it, Mildred," he added as he handed Jose the phone. Mildred wasn't leaving anything to chance when it came to Jose. She was determined never to let her out of her life again. She and Jose were the only two survivors from the Kyle family, and they both had two boys, as far as Mildred knew. But Jose would not be complete until she found her long-lost daughter.

"Hello, Mildred," Jose said. "So I see you decided to wake up with your scheming self," Mildred said. "Listen, you know my husband is timing our phone call right now, but I'll see you tomorrow," she added. "Okay. And Mildred," she pauses. Thanks for being my sister," she said. "Girl, you're about to make me cry, so hush up," Mildred replied. Their relationship was as good as it gets. They had formed a union that would never be broken. But Mildred's husband, Wally, was standing outside the bedroom listening to her conversation. And he wasn't too happy about his wife having a black sister with black kids coming around often. Not to mention that he would be entertaining a black family at the dinner table. But as it seemed, racism didn't have a chance of survival at the McCormick residence, whether Wally liked it.

The kids were worn out at the Mullins residence, and while Jose was putting them to bed, Mullins prepared his wife a nice bubble bath and a glass of wine. With the investigation ongoing and having to go back and forth, it had drained the Mullins family, and he'd like nothing more than to relax and, once again, live everyday life. So he sat on his bed, staring at the doorway and waiting for his wife to finish her bath. And when she walked into the room, it was more than he'd expected. Jose had prepared herself for her husband as if it were her first time. Her beauty left him speechless, and while his eyes were glued to hers, their bodies were suddenly fixed like magnets, one against the other. It was as if they were communicating in a foreign language that no one else could understand. But it was their time, and it was a night of one magical moment after the other. The following day they were awakened by Levi banging on the door. "Wake up. I want cereal," he shouted. "Welcome home, Mommy," Mullins said jokingly. "Yeah, right," she said as she rolled out of bed. While they prepared breakfast, the doorbell rang. It was Mildred. "What are you doing here so early? Don't you have work to do at home, woman? Mullins said as he hugged Mildred. "Don't pay him any attention," Jose said as she walked her sister to her car.

Chapter 10: The Groundkeeper's Death

While the two sisters made small talk, Mullins decided to call Dave for an update on the investigation. What he'd learned from the Bridges interview was shocking. The Grand Jury had indicted him for the murder of his girlfriend. But he told Dave that Sandy had complained about Senator Adam's sexual advances toward her. "According to what you're telling me, there's a possibility that she might have been raped before being strangled," Mullins said. "That's exactly what I'm saying," Dave replied. "Then you have to move quickly because she should've been examined like yesterday," Mullins replied. "I'm on it," Dave said. As it seemed someone was attempting to get rid of all evidence. Sandy's body was already buried, so the evidence of sexual assault, if any, would have been documented by the medical examiner. So Dave went to the medical examiner, hoping to find a credible lead on her death. When he walked through the front door, he noticed no one at the front desk. Suddenly the coroner came out and said: "I've been expecting someone from the police department, but no one has shown up until now." My name is Dr. Whitaker, he said.

"So may I see the report," Dave asked. When he saw the report, it was shocking. It revealed that the deceased, Sandy Broderick, had been sexually assaulted before being strangled. Dave was furious that no one even bothered to follow up on evidence that could have determined if the accused boyfriend, Mike Bridges, was the person responsible for the murder. He decided to call Mullins immediately. "Hey partner, we got problems," Dave said. "What did you find out," Mullins asked. "Good news is the coroner records show a sexual assault before the victim was strangled. But the bad news is she's already in the ground," he said. "Dammit," Mullins complained. "Then our best hope is that they preserved a sample from the rape kit," says Mullins. "Just hold what you got, and I'll catch a flight back as soon as possible," he added. Dave thanked Mr. Whitaker for help but did not want to alert him of their plans to search for DNA samples. He knew that the samples had been either destroyed or hidden. But Dave planned to wait for his partner and return with a search warrant.

Officer Mullins was eager to return to Alabama, but it was too risky to leave Jose this soon. So the following day, he had to call on his sister-in-law Mildred. "Hi, there, my dear sweet sister-in-law," Mullins says. "Okay, cut the crap, Robert and tell me what you want," Mildred replied. "I need you to watch Jose and the kids. I haven't told her yet, but the investigation has taken a big turn, and I can't say when I'll be back," he explained. Mildred could tell by his demeanor that he couldn't tell her the details, so she said: "Just tell me when you're leaving, and I'll pack a few things and stay with her."

"Thank you so much," he replied with relief. Mullins didn't know if he should mention his findings to Jose concerning the Senator's wife, who looked like her twin sister. He worried it might be too much, considering she'd just returned from the Learning Center. But when he told her he had to go back, she sensed the urgency and knew it was necessary. She also knew it was concerning her daughter and began pressuring him for answers. "I don't want to get your hopes up until I know for certain," he said. "Just tell me what you've found out and let me deal with my hopes," Jose replied. "Well, I saw this woman, and she looked, walked, and sounded exactly like you. Except she was a little more White," he added. "What do you mean by a little more White," she asked. "I mean, maybe a little bit lighter skin," Mullins explained. He went on to say that she was married to a powerful senator in Mobile, Alabama. And the bad news was that this senator was somehow tied to the kidnapping of Levi.

Oh my God," said Jose as she covered her mouth. "I've had dreams of my daughter, and in my dreams, she was married to an evil man," she added. "Where is she? I have to see her," said Jose as she became panicky. "Now, that's why I didn't want to tell you. You're going to have to calm down and tell no one," Mullins explained. "It could not only screw up the entire investigation but cause the senator to relocate. And we'd back to square one," he added. "At least let me come with you," Jose pleaded. "That might be a problem," says Mullins. "Why is that a problem," Jose asked. "Well, after her husband recognized me from a photo, he sent her and the kids on vacation the next morning." "Oh my God, I need to see her now," Jose said. "You can't come now, but when she returns, I promise to keep her in my sight until you meet her face to face," he said. Jose's face lit up like a candle because she knew that if Officer Mullins made her a promise, she could count on it. "Okay, then go," Jose said reluctantly. "I have to wait until Mildred gets here. I've asked her to stay until I return," Mullins said. "I am perfectly capable of taking care of myself," she replied. "But I'm not going to turn down an opportunity to spend a few days with my sister," she added with a smile. While Mullins went to the bedroom to pack a bag, Jose quickly got on the phone with Mildred. "Girl, I hope you're on your way," she said. "Just as soon as I finish a big pot of soup for Wally. He'll eat soup every day if I let him, " Mildred said jokingly. "Okay, I'll be waiting for you," Jose replied.

When Mildred arrived, Mullins gave her a thank-you hug and was on his way. "I'll walk Robert out to the car. Just put your bag in the guest room," she said. She hugged him tight as they approached the car and told him to be careful. "We need you back, and we need you back alive," Jose said with teary eyes. "Justice will prevail, and I'll be back with good news, and that's a promise," he replied. Jose returned to the house and found Levi and Bobby out of bed. They heard the voice of their Auntie Mildred, and it was game over. "If you guys think you're gonna stay up all night, think again," Jose said, smiling at Mildred, who was hugged up with the boys. "I have enjoyed having nephews," Mildred said while smiling. "Speaking of nephews, when will your sons be home," Jose asked. "Well, Terry is a junior, and Gary is a freshman. They're both at the University of Georgia and should be here for Thanksgiving," Mildred said. "And this will be a holiday that we will all remember," she added. As for Levi and Bobby, they could not get enough of Auntie Mildred, but they would not escape bedtime. "Ten minutes, boys, and lights out," said Jose. The two sisters talked for a while and decided to get some much-needed sleep.

When Mullins arrived at GBI headquarters, Michael and JoAnn Browning were with Captain Mack in his office. As he was about to knock on the door, he overheard Michael Browning say, "If it weren't for that nigger boy of yours, we wouldn't be in this mess." That's when Mullins opened the Captain's door and asked, "What mess and what nigger boy?" They were all speechless because they didn't know how much Mullins had heard. "Let me be the first to apologize for Mr. Browning's language," Captain Mack said. "He's a big boy Captain. Let him apologize for himself," Mullins replied. "Well, in that case, said Michael, please accept my apology." "Go jump off a cliff," Mullins responded as he walked over and whispered to the Captain. He then left for the airport. "That is one mouthy nigger," said Michael as Mullins left. "He may be mouthy, but I don't see him being anybody's nigger" JoAnn replied. "That you can count on," said Captain Mack, agreeing with JoAnn. "I think his arrogance is kind of sexy," JoAnn said, smiling at Michael as she left the office. "Careful there Michael," said Captain Mack. " JoAnn might have a taste for dark meat," he added. "Why don't you just go straight to hell, Mack" Michael responded angrily. When Michael walked out of the building, he saw JoAnn as she watched Officer Mullins walking to his car. "Well, Dammit JoAnn. If you've gone lust over the nigger, at least try not to be so obvious," he said. JoAnn was getting tired of all the racism and the trouble that it was causing her family.

When Mullins arrived at the airport, he called Dave to let him know that he was on his way back. "I should be there in a couple of hours, so pick me up," he said. Dave was at the airport right on time. On the way to the hotel, they discussed the sexual assault of the housekeeper and decided that her boyfriend, Mike Bridges, was most likely innocent. But proving it would be a problem without a sample from the rape kit. When they arrived at the hotel in Mobile, the desk clerk had a message for Mullins. It was a message from Attorney Gibbs and marked "Urgent." He handed the note to Dave. "Looks like we've struck a nerve, partner," said Dave. "I think we've struck more than a nerve," Mullins replied. "Get some sleep 'cause something tells me we will earn our money tomorrow," he added.

The following day the two detectives called Attorney Gibbs and met him at a coffee shop on Main Street. "Morning, counselor," said Mullins. "Morning, my ass, you sons of bitches have been a pain in my butt long enough," Gibbs replied. "Just keep it up, cowboy, because we don't give a rat's ass about your pains," Dave responded. "And just because you're in Alabama don't mean I won't slap your little ass into the future," he added. "Okay, guys, just hold on," Mullins interrupted. "We are all civilized here, so let's have a seat and talk." "I'm not sitting next to that pit bull," Attorney Gibbs said as he moved his chair. The three guys ordered coffee and donuts, and Attorney Gibbs got straight to the point. "My client, Senator Adams, is a very important man around here, and he feels that you two are harassing his family." "I guess we harassed them to the point that he sent her to Aruba," Mullins replied. "How in the hell did you know that," said Gibbs. "Come on now Snow Flake. You already got one ass whipping coming, so you need to calm down," Dave replied. Finally, Attorney Gibbs asked them what it would take for them to pack up and go back to Georgia. "If I didn't know better, I'd think you were trying to bribe law officers," Mullins said. "But I'll make you a deal. You tell those murdering, kidnapping bastards that I'm not leaving without all y'all in handcuffs," he added. Attorney Gibbs got up from the table and left without saying a word. It was clear that Mullins had hit the nail on the head. "Okay, partner. Let's go see if we can rattle the Senator's cage," Mullins said. They headed to Senator Adam's residence, and Attorney Gibbs was already there when they arrived. They knocked on the door and the new housekeeper, Shanice, answered. "May I help you?" "Yes, Mam, we would like a word with Senator Adams if he's available," said Officer Mullins. "Please wait here," she said. As she turned around, the Senator was already standing there; this time, he invited them inside. "Come on in, gentlemen," he said. "I've been expecting your return." "What can I get you? Perhaps some fried chicken or maybe some watermelon? Shanice, would you check the pantry for some watermelon? My nigger guest appears to be a bit hungry," he said as he winked his eye at Attorney Gibbs.

"We're here to investigate the death of your former housekeeper, Sandy Broderick, and the kidnapping of Levi Mullins. "Are you speaking of the little nigger boy that I read about in the papers" the Senator replied. "He seemed to be a sweet little nigger boy. Was he related to either of you" he asked. Dave saw that Mullins was furious and doing all he could to keep from pulling his service revolver. So he immediately took the lead and asked a few normal questions like when was the last time you saw her and what was she wearing when she left. He knew the Senator was doing all he could to make Mullins snap. If he could find one reason to file charges against them, it would be the end of the investigation. But Mullins maintained his composer while Dave conducted a standard questionnaire. When they left, Dave decided that he would drive. "Hey, partner are you okay," he asked. Mullins was quiet for a few minutes, and then he spoke. "We are going to nail that arrogant bastard, and he's going to help us do it," said Mullins. "Now that's the spirit partner," Dave replied.

It was time to pay another visit to the Coroner who did the autopsy on Sandy Broderick. When they arrived, they saw him suddenly disappear behind the window. "You go around back, and I'll knock on the front door," Officer Mullins said. As he knocked on the door with no answer, the good coroner was exiting the rear entrance only to be greeted by Dave. "Going somewhere, Doc," Dave asked. "I was about to leave," said the coroner. "Well, I can see that, but we were hoping to talk with you about the Broderick girl. Hoping you could tell us more about the rape kit and the samples under her fingernails," Dave said. Immediately the coroner became a little edgy about how much the detective knew. "I had nothing to do with her death," he said. "Why don't we go back inside and talk about it," Dave said. The coroner was unaware that Dave had no actual knowledge of either rape or samples from the victim's fingers. But it did spark a conversation that might lead to a confession from Dr. Whitaker. When they entered, Dave opened the front door for Mullins. "Okay, partner, the good coroner was just about to tell us about the deceased," Dave said. "I'm all ears," Mullins replied. The Coroner, Dr. Whitaker, started telling all that he knew while Dave and Mullins listened with a careful ears. He began by stating that Attorney Gibbs and two other guys had come by and told him to cremate the body. He said he informed Attorney Gibbs of the suspected rape and DNA tissue under her fingernails. And even with that knowledge, Attorney Gibbs demanded the samples and the rape kit. "That's against the law, and you could be in serious trouble, Dr. Whitaker," Mullins explained. "No, No, No, I gave them only one of the samples. I always keep a sample in case it's lost," he replied. "Well, in that case, where is it," Dave asked. "It's in the safe. I'll get it," he replied. He opened the safe and paused as if he were having second thoughts. Suddenly he pulled out a handgun, turned, and fired at the officers. As they fell to the floor, Dave returned fire, striking the coroner in the chest area. He hurried over to try and save his life, but the good doctor didn't make it. With his last breath of air, he whispered to Dave, "Senator Adams strangled the housekeeper and broke her neck after he raped her." Dave was shocked to hear the coroner's confession. He stood up to remove the second set of samples and the rape kit from the safe and bagged them as evidence. However, he kept the coroner's confession to himself until he and his partner could figure out who they could trust. Dave knew for sure that there were police officers in Mobile still on Boss's payroll, and he had to be careful. When the local police arrived, they confiscated the samples and the rape kit from the two GBI agents. Dave asked the Captain of the SWAT team to make sure of the chain of custody for the samples and the rape kit because he knew it was the only thing connecting Senator Adams to the murder of Sandy Broderick.

When Officers Mullins and Dave returned to their hotel, they decided to have dinner. But as soon as he sat down, they received a call from the SWATT Captain. The groundskeeper had come to the station and requested to speak with the GBI from Georgia. He had information concerning the death of the deceased housekeeper Sandy. Dave and Mullins rushed down to the station, and the Senator's groundskeeper told them that he had witnessed the Senator through a window fighting with Sandy on the day she was murdered. "I see him grab her around the neck and choke her," said Garcia. "But I don't know if she was dead," he added. Dave asked if he could show them where this incident happened and where he was when he saw it. Garcia agreed to meet them the following day. However, he was instructed not to talk to anyone else about what he'd seen. Mullins immediately asked the Captain to obtain a search warrant for the Senator's home. So the groundskeeper, Garcia, headed back to Senator Adam's home, where he lived in the employee quarters. He had no idea he'd made a fatal mistake by returning to the property after leaving the police station. Someone at the station called the Senator and told him that Garcia had come to the station and talked to the GBI from Georgia. No doubt it was a dirty cop among those on Boss's payroll.

Attorney Gibbs was called immediately and informed of the situation. The Senator told Gibbs that Garcia had to disappear before daybreak. Attorney Gibbs agreed and said the Senator to set the house alarm, not exit. It would allow him to use the alarm system as an alibi. The night was quiet until midnight when two of Attorney Gibb's accomplices arrived in a black van. They returned to the employee quarters, where they found Garcia sound asleep. They knocked on the door and said that they were the police. Garcia thought it was Dave and Mullins and opened the door. When he realized it was trouble, it was too late. One of the men grabbed him around the neck, and with one quick twist, his neck was broken and his body lifeless. Garcia had lost his life trying to do the right thing. As the two henchmen loaded his body into the van, the evil Senator watched from his bedroom window. His alibi would be ironclad because the alarm system would show that he never came out of his home after 6 pm. And Garcia was last seen alive at the police station after 7 pm. The two men took Garcia's body to the boat dock, where he was stuffed in a 50-gallon drum mixed with cement. The container was taken far from the shore and dropped into the bottomless waters.

The following day Dave and Mullins arrived early at the station. "Okay, guys, rise and shine. I need that search warrant like yesterday," said Officer Mullins. He was in an excellent mood because he knew that everybody involved was about to be exposed and indicted. "Here's your warrant Lone Ranger," says the desk Sargent. "Screw you very much," Dave replied as they reviewed the warrant, ensuring it was in order with proper signatures. "It's all there," said the Sargent with a sarcastic tone. The search crew was assembled and ready to follow Dave and Mullins to the Senator's home. When they got there, they knocked on the door and the new housekeeper, Shanice, answered it. "We have the warrant to search the premises, mam. If you would please let the Senator know that we're here. "He's still in bed. It doesn't appear that he even left his room all evening," she said. "But I'll let him know you're here," she added. Shortly after, the Senator came to the door wearing his robe and a big grin. "Morning, gentlemen. What gives me the pleasure of once again entertaining my favorite police officers, Barney and Andy from Mayberry?" As Officer Mullins handed him the warrant, he asked: "Where is Garcia?" "Why do you need to see Garcia" the Senator replied. "What the hell. Feel free to visit with him in the employee quarters out back," he said with a grin. Officer Mullins knew exactly what the grin meant and quickly returned to find Garcia's quarters empty. No sign of Garcia meant trouble. It had dirty cop written all over it. "Okay, guys, I need some pictures of this room, including the closets. And a full inventory of clothing and personal items. While the search team roped off Garcia's living quarters and took inventory, Mullins rushed back around the front to speak with the Senator about the whereabouts of Garcia. The Senator responded, "I don't know where he is, but if he's not here soon, he's fired." "You are one sick, evil bastard," said Mullins. "You can check my alarm system if you're doubting my integrity," the Senator replied. "Right, and I just bet it shows you never left the inside of your home," Mullins responded. "Damn, you are a good detective," the Senator said. When the guys finished with the photos and inventory of Garcia's living quarters, they told them to wrap it up. Meanwhile, Dave decided to take a look around inside the residence. He remembered that Garcia told them he'd witnessed the Senator through a window as he fought with Sandy. And there was only one window which was low enough to view the inside. And that window just happened to be the Senator's private study. When Dave entered the room, he looked down and noticed several scuff marks on the hardwood. He called for Mullins, and when he saw the scuff marks, they agreed that they were consistent with a scuffle described by Garcia. The nervous Senator Adams watched as they took photos of the flooring. Finally, they were finished and left the property. The Senator immediately called Attorney Gibbs and told him about the scuff marks. "Just have the damn flooring replaced before the bastards get another warrant for shoe marks," Gibbs said jokingly. "You're laughing, but that's exactly what they're gone do. Get the flooring guys out here right now," Senator Adams said as he angrily threw a glass vase against the wall. The floors were replaced within two hours, and the old flooring was removed and burned.

And just as the Senator predicted, Officer Mullins and Dave did return the next day with a warrant to test the flooring for shoe marks. When they arrived and served the warrant, Dave noticed that the flooring had been replaced and asked: "Where is the old flooring material, Senator?" "Your guess is as good as mine, Sherlock," he answered. It was too late. The floors had been replaced, and there was no way to prove that the scratches from the shoe marks matched the shoes belonging to the deceased Sandy Broderick. "You evil bastard," Officer Mullins said as he grabbed the Senator by his collar. "Careful now, detective. It seems you're looking for an assault charge," the Senator responded with a grin. "Just let it go, Mullins," said Dave as he removed his partner's hands from the Senator's neck. "You saw that detective, and I'm pressing charges. That black bastard just attacked me, so do your job and cuff him," the angry Senator shouted. "For what? I didn't see anything," Dave said. As they left the property, the new housekeeper, Shanice, looked on as if she had something to say. But it was not the time or place to ask questions with tempers flared, so the dynamic duo from Georgia headed back to the station. When they left, Shanice pulled out a cell phone and called an unknown person to tell them that the two GBI from Georgia had left the promises. As it turns out, Shanice was an undercover FBI agent assigned to investigate Senator Sam Adam's criminal activities, including the murder of the former housekeeper Sandy. "Get in here, Shanice," shouted the angry Senator. "What do you need, sir," she asked. "I need some ice in this bucket. I think I'll have a victory drink," he added as he slapped her buttocks while handing her the ice bucket. She turned and looked at him as if she wanted to tear his arm off, but she didn't want to blow her cover. She could hardly wait to put him in handcuffs. Finally, the Senator had met his match and didn't even know it. Shanice Sidney was one of the bureau's top self-defense instructors who would've liked nothing more than to rip his tongue out for all the nasty things he'd heard him say. She had recorded every phone conversation, including the one he made with the henchmen who murdered Garcia. But she didn't hear the recording until the following day and couldn't get him in protective custody. The house alarms would have alerted the Senator if she had opened the door to check on him. While her assignment was to uncover criminal activities between the Senator and his father-in-law, Jack Wallace, aka Boss, she had discovered so much more. And she knew that it was only a matter of time before the charge of attempted rape would be added to the list. Only this time, she would take care of his taste for dark meat once and for all.

Chapter 11: Deidre's Luck Runs Out

Meanwhile, when Officers Mullins and Dave arrived at the station, the desk Sargent told Mullins that his wife had called with an urgent message. As it appeared, Deidre had struck again. Only this time, José caught her in the act of breaking. When he called home, the police were still at the residence. "What's going on, José," he asked. "Well, Deidre decided she wanted to visit, except she chose the window instead of the door." "What," Mullins said in shock. "You heard me right. She chose the window instead of the door, and I helped her inside," José replied. "Oh my God, José, what did you do," he asked. "Before or after I whipped her ass," José asked? "Give me the damn phone, José," Mildred said. "How about asking if your wife is ok instead of worrying about this crazy lunatic Deidre" she shouted. "We're on our way home tonight, and thanks for being there for José," said Mullins. "Don't mention it. She's my sister, right" Mildred replied before handing the phone back to José. "Honey, we're taking the first flight out tonight," he said as he looked over at Dave. By now, Dave had heard enough to know that Deidre was in trouble, and it was time for Mullins to come clean. He explained everything Deidre had done to Dave over the past couple of weeks. Dave was in a state of shock. He didn't know whether to apologize or be angry that his partner didn't trust their friendship enough to tell him sooner. "I don't know why I didn't say something sooner. It's a difficult thing to tell your best friend, he said. "You mean you didn't know how to tell your best friend that his fiancée is a crazy slut" Dave replied. "Let's go get that flight home, man. I need a little recreational activity. But I will pay a visit to Deidre before seeing Ms. Sarah. With her fine self." Mullins could see that Dave was trying to mask his anger for Deidre, so he kept quiet and let him vent. He talked about everything except Deidre. "You do know that Librarians are sexy as hell, right," Dave said jokingly. "Man, you're crazier than I thought," Mullins responded with a sigh of relief.

When they arrived at the Atlanta airport, the Captain was there to meet them personally. "Okay, what have we done to earn a personal pickup from the good olé Captain Mack," Dave said jokingly. "Well, I didn't get a call from the governor of Alabama saying you guys had killed someone, so I decided to ensure no screw-ups at the airport," he replied. "Welcome back guys. I heard nothing but great things," he added. Jose was waiting with Bobby and Levi when they arrived at the station. Mildred had taken the liberty of going home to check on her husband, Wally. Of course, little Bobby and Levi shouted for joy as they ran and leaped into their father's arms. "Okay, guys say hello to Uncle Dave," Mullins said. Dave smiled as he realized how happy his partner was to see his family. He was still brokenhearted about his situation with Deidre, but he did his best to hide it. José hugged and thanked him for everything he did to help her husband. She also told him that he was not to blame for Deidre's actions and that he should do whatever he could to get her the medical attention she needed. "Go to her, Dave. She's at the hospital and lonely," Jose said. Dave nodded in agreement and told Mullins that he would call him tomorrow. He headed to the hospital to check on Deidre. Even though she had made bad choices, he knew she had no one else in the world to depend on. A policeman was sitting at her door when he arrived at the hospital. Dave opened the door slightly to peek inside and noticed Deidre's wrist was handcuffed to the bed rail. He asked the officer for the key and told him to take a break. He then went inside and unlocked the handcuffs. She looked at him with tears in her eyes. "I am so sorry for embarrassing you," she said. Dave didn't let her talk because he knew her actions were tearing her apart. "You don't have to explain. I know you regret all you've done, and the Mullins are good people who will open their hearts and forgive you." He sat by her side and put lotion on her hands and feet. It was apparent that Dave still had deep feelings for Deidre, but he knew that she would have to stand trial at some point for her actions. She had been charged with criminal trespassing, breaking with intent to do bodily harm, and, last but not least, attempted murder by way of substance abuse. Things were not looking good for Deidre. But Dave was there for her even though she had thrown him under the bus for a long-shot chance to be with his best friend and longtime partner, Officer Mullins. He sat by her bedside for the remainder of the night, trying desperately to find it in his heart to forgive. Throughout the night, he remembered how Mullins always talked about his father's teachings. And there was one thing in particular that ignited his memory. "If it's worth loving, it's worth forgiving." But to sit there and hold the same hand that turned you away was proving to be the hardest thing Dave had ever done. As he watched her lying there, his mind took him down memory lane and all the fun times they'd shared.

Meanwhile, the kids were asleep at the Mullin's house, and José was anxious to hear the news of her daughter. Finally, he told her that she would return with them to Alabama in three days as long as her sister Mildred was attending to the kids. José didn't know whether to be happy or sad. Whether to laugh or cry. It was the moment she'd waited for since her baby girl was taken from her arms by her evil father, Mr. Kyle. Almost unbelievable in every way. She looked at her husband, and tears of joy started to flow. She lay in his arms all night, afraid to fall asleep just in case it was a dream. Her eyes were wide open, and she determined that it would never end if it were a dream, even if it meant never sleeping again.

Chapter 12: Mother Daughter Reunion

Finally, the day had come for Dave and Mullins to return and finish what they had started. Only this time, José had gotten her to wish to tag along. Her sister, Mildred, was there to pick up her nephews, Bobby and Levi. "Yeah, let's get candy," Levi shouted. "Oh no, you don't, little fellow," José responded. "Scout's honor," Mildred said as she raised her left hand. "That's the wrong hand, Sis," José replied. "Anyway, we're leaving now, and Levi, no candy," she said, giving Mildred a tight hug. As Officer Mullins watched the two ladies do their sisterly love thing, he shook his head. "Oh, my God. Are y'all gone cry every time you hug" he asked. "And what if we do" Mildred responded with a smiley face. She was excited that José would finally get to hold her daughter again after thirty years. And now they were off for the Atlanta airport and on to the great state of Alabama.

When the plane landed in Mobile, Jose was so nervous that her hands were shaking. "Hey dude, you better get her to the hotel quickly," Dave said jokingly. "Just shut up, Dave," José replied as she anxiously waited to see her daughter. Mullins explained how everything would work when the three arrived at the hotel. First, she would have to wait until Dave gave the signal to approach her daughter. Then, after resting for a couple of hours in the hotel, they were off to the Mobile airport, where they would wait for the flight from Aruba. According to the airlines, Amanda Adams and her two kids would arrive within minutes. José had no idea what to expect. She remembered the harsh treatment of her father and the mean ways of his wife, Mrs. Kyle. The woman blamed her for giving birth to a baby girl ripped from her arms before she could give her a name. But now the time had come. José was only moments away from filling the space in her heart. An area reserved for over thirty years.

As they sat inside the airport waiting area, Amanda finally appeared with José's two grandchildren, Jaelin and Jody. As she came closer, there was no doubt in José's mind that this was her long-lost child. The Senator's driver met Amanda and the kids, and while he loaded the luggage, José's maternal instincts took complete control of her faculties. Dave tried to stop her, but it was too late. He grabbed Jose by her arm, but she turned to him angrily and said: "Let me go." Her eyes were filled with the wrath of an angry lioness preparing for battle to protect her young. The foreign nature of those three words, "Let me go," froze Dave in his tracks as Jose pressed her way to Amanda, where the two ladies stood face to face, staring each other down. Finally, Jaelin turned to her older brother Jody and said: "I'm scared." The kids were in a state of shock. It was as if they'd seen the ghost of their mother. Jose and Amanda were almost identical from head to toe. Even their voices were similar. Their eyes wandered up and down, gazing at each other as if they were in a place without space or time.

And then it happened. José spoke to her daughter as if she were whispering. "My name is José." Then, she paused to gather her strength and said louder, trembling, "My name is José, and I'm your mother." Amanda looked into José's eyes and saw her reflection. They gazed at each other for what seemed like an eternity. It was as if they'd read each other's mind, and with one spontaneous motion, they stretched out their arms and embraced. The moment seemed to have sucked all of the oxygen from the air. And refusing to let go, Amanda spoke with an identical whisper, "Mama." But as the tears began to flow like an endless river, she got louder and louder until her words rang loud and clear for the whole world to hear. "Mama," "Mama," she cried over and over as if she were a child speaking for the first time. And right there, in that magical moment where time stood still, they made a vow never to let go. As the news quickly spread throughout the airport of the mother-daughter reunion, the crowd gathered around and added more fuel to the fire with continuous applause. Officer Mullins struggled to maintain his composure but could not hold back the tears. He concluded José's strength was not in the success of overcoming her past but instead in her struggle to hold on to her child again.

As Dave watched from a distance, he knew there would be more challenges ahead for Jose. Her daughter, Amanda Adams, would be faced with the difficult decision of choosing between the only family she's ever known and her biological mother. As for Jose, she would have to find a way to accept Amanda's choice, regardless of her decision. It was no secret that Senator Adams was not the type of man who would accept Amanda's black mother as his mother-in-law. And there wasn't a chance in hell that her adoptive father, Jack Wallace, aka Boss, would even consider abandoning his racist views. Senator Adams and Boss were still being investigated for murder and kidnapping, and Officer Mullins would never consider closing the case on either until they were both behind bars. Even though Michael and JoAnn Browning knew the plan to kidnap his son, he was willing to look past their wrongdoings in exchange for their testimony against Jack Wallace. As for Dave's fiancé, Deidre, she'd been released from the medical facility and sent to the county jail, where she would wait for a pre-trial. He didn't know whether to help her or just let go. His heart was saying yes, but his mind kept telling him no. It was unthinkable that she would put the Rohypnol drug in Jose's drink. A horrible act of evil that could have caused severe memory loss for his best friend's wife. Not to mention trying to inject more of the same drug into her system during a visit while she lay helpless in the hospital. It would seem less complicated to forget her and rush to the loving arms of Sarah Jenkins from the adoption agency. But Dave still had feelings for Deidre that were deeply rooted in memories. Memories that would not let him turn his back and walk away.

But for Jose and her daughter Amanda, life was beginning. They clearly understood the past, but now their focus was on the future. But the grandkids, Jaelin and Jody, were still confused. The only grandparent they'd ever known was Grandpa Jack, who adopted Amanda when she was only three weeks old. His wife, Mrs. Ida Ruth Wallace, was dearly loved by everyone in Mobile, Alabama, until her death in the summer of 1946. She died while giving birth to a stillborn baby girl. They'd called her Amanda if it was a girl and Jack Jr. if it was a boy. Jack was devastated after losing his wife and child. His life was empty until he received a call from his cousin, Sheriff Wallace, in Jackson, Georgia. The Butts County Sheriff knew Mr. Kyle had recently put an illegitimate baby girl up for adoption at the Browning Adoption Agency. The old man had again failed to control his sexual appetite for young black girls. Only this time, it was his 14-year-old daughter that he'd held in captivity.

The same child that he and Dr. Lewis had taken from Josephine, the black housekeeper, in the winter of 1930. His wife, Mrs. Kyle, was fed up with his inability to control his sexual appetite, so she insisted that the infant be adopted immediately. She constantly complained that her home had become a breeding ground for darkies. Finally, it led to the secret transfer of the infant to the adoption agency under the name of Baby Jane Doe. The biological mother appeared on the birth certificate as Darkie Jane Doe. No one would ever know that the infant's mother was black. When Sheriff Wallace told Jack about the baby girl in Jackson, Georgia, he came the next day to adopt her and named her Amanda Wallace. The birth certificate at the courthouse remained as Jane Doe with hopes of burying her past. And for that reason, everyone involved with the adoption vowed never to reveal that Jose was the biological mother. Jack Wallace had always told Amanda that her mother had died giving birth. But now, thirty years later, the mother-daughter reunion had uncovered the dark secrets of the past.

Amanda wasted no time as she eagerly introduced her two children to their biological grandmother. Jaelen's eyes were filled with tears of joy, but Jody was a bit reluctant as he observed Officer Mullin's arm around Jose's shoulder. Then suddenly Amanda recognized Mullins and asked: "Aren't you the investigator who was at my home a while back?" "Yes, I am, and this is my partner Dave" he answered. Jose could sense Amanda's dislike for Mullins and quickly interrupted the conversation, hoping to change her mindset. It was almost as if she were pleading for her daughter's acceptance. "This is my husband Robert, and we have two small sons, Levi and Robert Jr." "How old are they," Jaelin asked? "Levi is three, and Robert Jr. is only two months old," she answered. "We call him Bobby," she added. "Why are they so young," Jody asked. "Okay, guys. Enough questions for now," Amanda interrupted. "Is there someplace we can talk privately?" Officer Mullins asked. "Sure, if you will follow me to my home," she replied. Officer Mullins could see that Jose's eyes were welling with tears at the thought of letting go of Amanda's arm. He knew he had to tell Amanda enough about the ongoing investigation to gain her trust. It was obvious that she and Jose were bonding at warp speed, and nothing was going to separate them ever again. Not even her husband, Senator Adams. So while Mullins secured the kids with the limo driver, Dave arranged to use the airport security office for the short briefing. Amanda listened carefully as Officer Mullins explained that Senator Adams and her father, Jack Wallace, were suspects in the investigation. He told her that the most important thing she needed to remember was that Jose's life could be in danger while in Mobile, Alabama. He also said that Jose couldn't go to her home because the Senator was a suspect in kidnapping their three-year-old son, Levi. "Why would anyone kidnap a three-year-old child," Amanda asked. "They took him hostage to make Jose stop her search for the child taken from her at birth," Mullins replied. "Oh, my God. I'm that child," Amanda said as she turned to her mother in shock. "And now your mother's safety depends on you being silent until this investigation is over." "Can we count on your silence, Mrs. Adams?" Dave asked? "Yes, of course, but when will I see her again," Amanda asked. "I promise it won't be long if you just trust me," Mullins answered. Jose's tears started to flow at the thought of losing sight of her daughter again. She did not want to let Amanda out of her sight, but she knew it was the only way. "I am so happy that I've found you, and I will never lose you again," Jose said. Amanda responded with an ever-so-soft whisper to her mother, "Thanks for never giving up on me." Dave escorted Amanda to the limo while Mullins walked with Jose to the parking deck.

When the limo left the airport, Dave suddenly remembered that the kids were never briefed. And it was almost sure that Jody would tell Senator Adams that his grandma Jose was at the airport. "Let's go, guys," Dave said. "What's the rush" Mullins replied.

"The kids will tell the Senator about seeing Jose," Dave responded. "You're right," said Mullins as he hurried Jose to the hotel. And just like Dave had predicted, the first words out of Jody's mouth were, "We saw our Grandma Jose at the airport, right Mom?" Senator Adams looked at his wife and froze in his tracks. It was terrible news, and he knew the worst was coming. "Is that right, son?" he jokingly replied, gazing sharply at Amanda. Usually, he would welcome his wife home with a hug and kiss, but this time he hurried to his office and closed the door. The GBI team from Georgia had finally unlocked the secrets of his wife's past, and there was no way to undo the damage. It could cost him his family and his political bid for the Governor's office.

He immediately called Attorney Gibbs and informed him that Amanda's birth mother was in Mobile. And to make matters worse, she'd been formally introduced to Amanda and the kids. "Stay calm, and don't tell Amanda anything. In the meantime, I'll call Boss and figure out a way to make them all disappear for good," Attorney Gibbs said. Amanda sensed something was wrong, so she followed her husband to his office. "Open the door, Sam. We have to talk," she said. When he didn't open the door, she shouted. "Open the damn door, Sam, right now!" Finally, Senator Adams opened the door and asked Amanda to sit down. He told her that her father was to blame for everything and that he was an innocent party. He was so convincing that Amanda had tears welling in her eyes and believed every word he'd said. She turned all of her anger on her father, Jack Wallace, for keeping her from the truth. She was angry and disappointed that he'd kept her from her biological mother for over thirty years. She felt robbed of her childhood, and nothing could make up for the loss because the question still lingered. Who is Amanda?

Chapter 13: The Take-Down

When Boss got wind of the news, he rushed to talk with Amanda. He had no idea that his crooked son-in-law had blamed everything on him. Amanda was so angry that she called Jack a monster and locked herself in her bedroom. "What in God's name did you tell her, Sam," he asked. The Senator had no words except "I had no choice but to blame it all on you." "You sneaky little bastard. I should cut your tongue out," Boss replied in anger. "Well, it is your damn fault," the Senator responded. The two men had no idea that the new housekeeper, Shanice, was an undercover FBI agent who was eavesdropping and recording the entire conversation. They even discussed the murder of Garcia and how they planted Sandy Broderick's body in the trunk of Mike Bridges' car. Shanice had enough evidence on the two men to get a conviction, but she needed more on the money laundry and bank fraud case. As she turned away from the door, Attorney Gibbs stood right behind her. "Were you eavesdropping on the Senator?" he asked. Shanice tried to leave, but he grabbed her by the arm and yelled out to Boss. When Boss and Senator Adams came out of the room, Gibbs told them that he'd caught the housekeeper with her ear to the door. Shanice knew she couldn't afford to have her pockets searched, so she snatched away from Gibbs and ran through the kitchen. "Leave me alone, Mister," she screamed.

Amanda heard the scream and came out of her bedroom. "What in the hell is going on out here," she asked. "Nothing is going on except your nosey housekeeper just got caught eavesdropping on your Dad and the Senator," Attorney Gibbs replied. Amanda rushed out back and found Shanice in the employee quarters crying. "What did they do to you, Shanice," she asked. "That lawyer fellow grabbed me by the arm because I was standing at the door. I wanted to clean Mr. Adam's office, but they were arguing about something," she replied. "That's when that lawyer fellow said I was eavesdropping, but I wasn't Mrs. Adams," she added. "Well don't you worry none, and I'll take care of Gibbs," Amanda said. "Why don't you just take the rest of the day off." "Thank you so much, Mam," Shanice replied with a sigh of relief.

When Amanda left the employee quarters, Shanice reached into her pocket and checked her recording device. The recording was as clear as a bell with details of Garcia and Sandy's murder. It was certainly enough to clear Sandy's fiancé of his murder charge. Shanice knew she had to leave the property with the recorder before she went back into the main house, so she hurried to her car and drove to the FBI substation. Her visits to the substation were usually after dark and only in emergencies, but the information she'd recorded was far too important to risk losing. When she played the recording at the station, they were shocked that Boss Wallace would be so careless. It was almost unbelievable that he or the Senator would even utter the recorded words. Shanice had done excellent work, but there was still a possibility they knew she was undercover. Attorney Gibbs had caught her eavesdropping at the door, but he didn't know how much she'd heard. Her continued surveillance was risky, but she had a personal debt to settle with the Senator. He had developed a habit of slapping her on the butt at every chance. Each time she would visualize breaking his arm and watching him suffer. When the FBI team informed Captain Mack of the evidence obtained by their undercover agent, he immediately contacted Officer Mullins and Dave and told them to wrap it up and come home. This was bad news for Jose because she wanted to spend more time with her daughter. But there was no way Mullins could allow her to go to Amanda's home, so he and Dave needed to be a part of the takedown. They asked Captain Mack for permission to join the Mobile Task Force and the FBI, and he agreed. But only if Jose is in police protection. "You make damn sure that the FBI has Jose in protective custody, and I'm on my way," Captain Mack said. Officer Mullins explained the terms of the agreement to Jose, and she reluctantly agreed. She had no concern for her safety but was afraid for Amanda and her grandkids. "Will my baby be alright," she asked. "I give you my word that I will make sure they're out of harm's way," Mullins responded.

He and Dave arrived at the FBI substation just as they were directed by Captain Mack and placed Jose in protective custody. Then, after a short briefing with the Mobile Task Force, they went to the Senator's home with arrest warrants for the murder of Garcia. All other charges would be added at a later date because there was a chance that Shanice's cover had been blown. And if so, the three men might take flight before being arrested. Even though the undercover FBI agent, Shanice Sidney, had been given the day off by Mrs. Adams, she was not going to miss this for the world. So when she got word that they were closing in for an arrest, she returned to the substation. "Okay, fellows, I'm present and accounted for," she said jokingly. "We're wrapping it up, Agent Sidney," the FBI team leader responded. "Come on now, Captain. This is my show, and it looks like show time to me," Shanice replied. "What the hell. Okay, everybody listens up. Agent Sidney is going to the residence undercover. We move in on her command. Okay, Shanice, it's your show, so don't be a hero".

When she arrived, Amanda reminded her that she had off the rest of the day. Shanice told her she was there to pick up some items from the employee quarters. Amanda told her she would be with the kids for a while. "A little shopping will ease my mind," she said. This was perfect timing for serving the arrest warrants. Agent Sidney watched as the driver left the property with Mrs. Adams and her two kids. She made contact and told the team to get ready. As she walked through the house, she stopped at the Senator's office and noticed that Senator Adams, Boss, and Gibbs were having drinks and talking loudly. She knocked on the door and entered the room, and as usual, Senator Adams was all liquored up. She intentionally walked close enough for him to take one last swing at her butt. And when he took the bait, she broke his arm and gave the "All Clear" signal for the team to enter the residence. Gibbs tried to take her down, but she broke his jaw. As for Boss, he'd seen enough and tried to run, but the FBI agents were at every exit.

The three men were arrested and charged with conspiracy and the murder of Garcia, whose body was never recovered. When Officer Mullins noticed Senator Adams holding his arm and Attorney Gibbs with a swollen jaw, he asked the FBI agent what happened. The agent smiled and said, "Ask Agent Sidney. She would be the young lady sitting with the Captain, trying to convince him that it was self-defense." Officer Mullins glanced at Senator Adams and Attorney Gibbs as they received medical attention. He found it hard to believe Agent Sidney had caused all that damage. When they walked past her, Dave decided to try his luck with a wink. Officer Mullins told him he'd better take a good look at the Senator and Attorney Gibbs.

The next day Jose visited her daughter Amanda at her home. All she could do was try and comfort her at a time when her entire world seemed to have fallen apart. Her husband and father were both charged with conspiracy and murder. The kids were sad that their father was in jail, which worsened matters. No one knew whether Senator Adams and Boss would receive political favors or be indicted and found guilty of the crimes. But at least Jose had seen her daughter, and the bad guys were behind bars.

Would Jose and Amanda be able to unite their families and enjoy a life of racial harmony? Who knows? Perhaps *Whites Only*.

www.ingramcontent.com/pod-product-compliance
Lightning Source LLC
LaVergne TN
LVHW011937070526
838202LV00054B/4690